Uncle To

No doubt you will nave heard of the famous story Uncle Tom's Cabin. Well, my Uncle Tom who lived in Donegal, Ireland's second largest county, didn't have a cabin but he did have a cabinet in his cottage. His Cabinet of Curiosities he called it. There, any potential resemblance to the other Uncle Tom you would think might end and you'd be right. He wasn't a slave, though as a young man he had been in service at the Big House. One of those Anglo Irish ascendancy houses much maligned as the incarnation of feudal British rule in Ireland. They were called 'Big' as a reference to their size and the level of influence they had over the encircling environment. The tenants of the Big House estates used the term as a comparison between their humble dwelling and the often massive and sumptuous residences of the Anglo-Irish aristocracy.

The house, a fine example of Tudor Revival, was built on an earlier site. It wasn't big relative to others on the island of Ireland but relative to the standard Donegal cottage it was immense. At one time it controlled over ten thousand acres but this had been reduced to one thousand by 1906. It had tall steep roofs and gables with mullioned and dormer windows and a square turret next to the servant's wing. Its location above Lough Dunlewy was breathtaking.

As was common, the Ascendancy family, five generations of them, finally fell into debt and the house passed into the hands of retired Major General Reginald George Cathcart Grelee, late of the 9th Deccan, India. He returned from Hindustan following Kitchener's Indian army reforms of 1903, with an entourage of punkahwallah in tow. It was rumoured the housekeeper, Mrs Singh, was his native wife. He had gone native in the hot Indian sun. Having commanded some vassal state in North West India, where a small raj's fortune had come his way for turning a blind eye to the excesses of the local Raja. He swanned around in a Musselman's dress, with hennaed hands and wore an Indian mustachios. Being a colonial invader it seemed only right and proper to take a cut of the Raja's worth and run. He ran to Ireland rather than Blighty, bringing his fortune, retinue and violence with him. For he was an argumentative, violent man.

Mrs Singh had a daughter, Eva. Half cast they said. As if she was some inferior sort of moulding. Low quality seconds. Like the set of crockery my Ma kept for special occasion, bought in Hector's hardware half price. The plates having failed in the kiln, the heat leaving them slightly warped on one edge. Like Eva warped in the heat of passion between the Major General and Mrs Singh.

Uncle Tom, or Tomas was on my Ma's side of the fence. His family could trace their roots to good land in County Kildare, "the thoroughbred county". They had been moved west during the plantation years. To hell or Connaught had been Cromwell's cry. Not having a compass Tom's lot ended up in Ulster, up among the "Hills People" and Red O'Neill. He said, despite his family living in Donegal for three hundred years he was still a blow in to some "Donegalians".

I hadn't been there in years. Dun na nGall means Fort of the Foreigner. Appropriate given Tom's experience.

His cottage was perched on the edge of Lough Dunlewy, a few miles from the village with a similar name. While Donegal is a county in the Province of Ulster, it is not part of the wee black North.

It is Irelands County of contradictions, cold beaches, soft rain, hard grasses, murderous waters, harsh beauty. It is a county of ethereal beauty. The wild child, beaten by the North Atlantic, its edges chiselled ragged and broken like Shane McGowan's teeth. And what a glorious sound its beauty makes. The sound of the earth in harmony. Buttercups and Bogwort swaying like Pans People in a trance like state. The sweet smells rising up from golden sands and heather bogs. Smells laced with intent like Chanel No 5. And lakes, like glass in a windless hour, turned to snarling shards of broken panes on a soft day. The March Hare sane in his domain and above little dinosaurs, Guillemots and Kittiwakes swoop and cry.

On earlier visits waking as a child, my brothers the double D's, Damien and Declan, would prop me up on the windowsill of the meagre little annex room that passed for our bedroom in the cottage. The windowsill's timber roughly hued but rubbed smooth by pride. A small window, more hacked than built in the two feet thick wall, looked out over his meagre stone strewn garden towards Errigal. Mount Errigal cone shaped and screed covered. The screed running down her face like tears. Like oul mother Ireland, Cathleen ni Houlihan weeping for her four green fields.

'It's like the dunces hat Mrs Sullivan made us wear in her class,' Declan had observed.

Standing two thousand four hundred feet, it is the highest peak in the Derryveagh Mountains and the tallest in Donegal. The highest and steepest of the Seven Sisters, she blushes like a big girls blouse as the pink crystals in the quartzite rock are ignited by the setting sun.

The four panes in the cottage window, often opaque with condensation, was our window onto history. The glass a hundred years old, borrowed from the Big House Tom said. It was as if by looking through its grains of sand we were putting a lens on the past. The vision of a distant age. A slower more deliberate time, where the waking day was guided by the raw basic human needs of sustenance and warmth and community. When news from over the brow of the

4

next hill was national news. When word came from the next cottage of their family living in the "States", it was reason for a gathering of the clan. Like the reporting of some alien world.

It was the 1960's then. The age of free love, ban the bomb, swinging London, the Cold War, Wendy's burgers and the E Type Jag. Yet in this place none of that mattered. It was of interest but that was the world of the big smoke, the poor emigrant, the foreign government. A strange world enticing, swallowing up the young, the needy and the ambitious. Leaving the old to labour beyond reasonable years. Leaving the methods and the processes of their time set in a soft jelly. The aspic of age. Like the forerunner to living museums. Left with their peat bogs and outside loos.

The cottage was of stone construction, low and lean. Whitewashed as was the tradition. The original thatch of reeds, having been replaced by a heavy slate roof on one half, twenty years earlier. The external wall surface, like other Donegal contradictions was smoothly rough. The layers of calcimine slaked lime whitewash, built up over a hundred years, giving the surface a white pearlescent finish. To the front there were four windows, two on either side of a low broad door. The door split in two. Painted glossy roaring red, it was like a Colleen's first blush. Facing south, it would keep children in and animals out. The cottages, generally being small and damp, the top half could be thrown open to allow light and air in. It aided air circulation given the prevalence of smoke from the large hearth fire. On our arrival, Tom would be seen leaning over the bottom half, pipe in hand or mouth, the epitome of contentment. The threshold stone beneath his feet centrally, sculptured into a smooth concave wave by the feet of family, friends and landlord agents over its two hundred years of existence. Life and its paraphernalia carried in, death and the paranormal carried out.

To the left of the front door, a lean to corrugated shed, to the far right a stone built add on housed the "shitter" and the pigsty. Each with a narrow wooden door hung on heavy metal swing bars.

The doors with eight inch gaps top and bottom. That's to let the smell of shite out, Tom would pronounce with emphasis on the word shite. Designed to make the children giggle and my Ma blush. His face screwed up with devilment.

He was a tall gangly man, his skin leather like and parched. His arms and general stance sinewy and powerful. Sculptured in to bog oak by seventy plus years of toil. His face had the hue of the Mediterranean, like one of those Spaniards of the great armada who found themselves shipwrecked and landlocked in Kinnagoe Bay. In contrast, he sprouted a fine head of luminescent white hair and matching beard. His head and face appeared to be in a state of constant turmoil, like the Atlantic waves smashing into the rocky coast at Slieve League. It was hard to say what he looked like under the beard but it was rumoured, he was the image of Richard Harris in his youth.

The beard yellowed around his mouth and to the right hand side by tobacco smoke. For he was a great pipe smoker. My Ma said, there wasn't another man in Donegal who could smoke a pipe with more skill and style than Uncle Tom. On occasion Donegal got stretched to the Province of Ulster and on one occasion the island of Ireland. In that she was probably right. There was a causal serenity about the way he smoked. It was different from Grandad Barry, his pipe smoking was a ritual honed over years. Toms was a natural talent. He claimed he first pulled a pipe when nine year old. A little cracked Knockcroghery clay, shaped like a question mark. He found and secreted it on his person after a wake at Winnie McFaddens house. He had gone there to lead his grandfather Eamon home, him being virtually blind.

He kept that pipe among many other trinkets in his Cabinet of Curiosities. The cabinet being wholly at odds with its surroundings. Tall and elegant it reached to the ceiling of the good room. Crafted from a dark foreign wood, the grain skilfully cut to create mirror image finishes. The bottom half being of a solid construction with two locking doors. On top, the unit was stepped back creating a small shelf at waist level. Out of this could be drawn a deeper shelf, supported on two extendable arms. The arms being pulled in to position by two small ornate brass handles. The purpose being, the collected and stored curiosities could be taken out and examined or simply displayed on the shelf. The shelf, when extended, allowed the user to sit comfortable in front of the cabinet using it like a desk. The cabinet took pride of place in the good room, which was located between the kitchen and the main bedroom. There were no halls in the cottage and you passed through the good room on the way to the bedroom.

On entering the cottage, you walked straight in to the kitchen living room, which encompassed one space. There were two window, one on the front wall to the right of the door and a second opposite it on the back wall. Both small, they let in limited light. Standing in the doorway facing in, a door to your right led to the annex room, where we took up residence. A door to your left and a single step up, took you to the good room. Unlike the bedroom and good room, the kitchen and annex had no ceilings. These rooms opening to the timber joists and roofing reed above.

The partition wall, between the annex and the kitchen, was taken up by the stone hearth, its stark stone sides rising up and tapering off at the top like a Bishop's Mitre. It's opening so large a man could comfortably sit within it on either side of the fire.

Five rough wooden shelves to its left held cooking pots and pans. Directly opposite stood a pine wooden dresser, which had a single top mounted display shelf. On this sat four or five large oval plates of varying styles. They had been salvaged from the Big House after its demise.

This was the house of the Major General, burnt down by the IRA in 1921. During the so called disturbances. He had died five years earlier leaving Eva and her mother, Mrs Singh, comfortable but isolated. A few years later, the mother returned to her family in India. Eva, half caste, half English, half child, was an easy target. It was said local volunteers refused to partake in the rampage that fateful night. It was told how some including Tom, then a young man, had gone to the house to warn Eva of the impending assault. They had offered to remove items for safe keeping but did not offer to defend the house against attack. Tom said she was unmoved by their pleas to leave the house. Defiant, not in an arrogant manner but in a sort of resigned way. That somehow her life was predestined and what would happen was the will of God. It was not clear which God, as it was rumoured the house had several little secret shrine erected to various

Indian deities. Tom said it was a black stain on the county. A defenceless woman dying in the defence of her home. He never used the word murdered but she surely was murdered. It transpired after her death,

Eva had been selling off much of the content of the house and giving the proceeds to local worthy causes. She did not want it known as she feared locals would decline the assistance, thinking it the charity of the conqueror. She was given a low key Christian burial and rests in the ground at the Church of the Scared Heart overlooking the lough.

I was told there was some debate as to whether she could be buried in consecrated ground, as no one was sure she was a Christian, never mind a Catholic. The Major was an Presbyterian and the mother a Hindu. Eva was found with a set of Rosary Beads around her neck. Despite having been struck by a rifle bullet, she had managed to drag herself into an East West alignment, in keeping with the alignment of the Sacred Heart chapel, three miles away as the crow flies. These facts would later prove significant in the decision to give her a Christian burial. Father Murphy, a tyrant of a man from Tipperary, was not convinced at first. But Mrs Doherty, a woman who had done service at the Big House during the Majors time, gave evidence to a committee of three, that she had seen Eva on occasion in her bedroom, on her knees. That was enough for two of the three and they voted for poor Eva to be given a modest plot left of the chapel gate. Driven by a guilty conscience some had sniped.

Father Murphy was not so easily swayed, until word came from a local Solicitor, local being Letterkenny, that Eva had intended to leave a bequest of one hundred pounds for repair of the local church roof. This was a princely sum in its day. Enough to buy you through the Pearly gates and the first stage of sainthood. There was one problem, she didn't specify which church. The RC church, which nurtured and cared for the vast majority of the local population being the Sacred Heart. The local Protestant church, bereft of a congregation, was a few miles farther on. The Major, when he went to church, which was three times a year, Easter, Christmas Day and on his birthday, always attended St Euans. The church being opened especially for this latter hallowed occasion. In tow, would be an entourage of Indian staff, one or two local Presbyterian families and Eva. Never Mrs Singh. An ecumenical debate ensued. In the meantime, the Catholics got her in the ground, on the basis possession is nine tenths of the law.

A conclave of local dignitaries was assembled to represent RC interests. The Reverend Samuel Gamble, whose remit covered several Protestant parish churches and an ever declining congregation, represented St Euans. The third son of a well to do land owner in Meath, he had taken the normal ordination path, studying theology at Trinity College, Dublin with a Masters in Divinity at the Selwyn Divinity School at Cambridge. Having aspired to something less isolated, he found himself in Donegal fighting a rear-guard action against the march of Republicanism. The matter caused quite a stir and even made front page news in the Derry Journal. The meeting of Christian minds took place in a hotel in Dunfanaghy, it being deemed a neutral venue. It was clear from the start, despite the courtesies paid to each side by the other, it was going to be a titanic struggle. The outcome was to be of a similar nature to that much vaunted tragedy.

It was clear from evidence given by local builders that the roofs on both churches were in dire need of repair.

The Solicitor, a Mister O'Hanlon, confirmed Eva's attendance at his offices on 3rd of July, 1921. He recalled, she had mentioned something about visiting town for a new hat. She had not specified which church. She had mentioned several people and bequests as a precursor to preparing a will. Perhaps, some sort of premonition on her part, he speculated. He was to prepare a draft will. It had been arranged he would call on her later in the year, on a date to be notified to him, to complete the list of bequests and finalise the will. He mentioned only in passing that a small fee of one pound fifteen shillings was outstanding for the work done. He was assured by both sides the sum would be paid from the bequest.

The Reverent Gamble produced receipts for the purchase of five galvanised buckets, bought the previous winter. The crucial point being, Eva had donated the small sum for their purchase. This, the Reverent argued, was a clear indication of her state of mind and knowledge as to the state of St Euans roof. Her attendance at his church on at least twenty occasion and her name clearly written three times in the churches visitor's ledger, were irrefutable evidence of her close connection and devotion to his church. He could not explain the presence of the Rosary Beads. He certainly never saw her wearing them. His evidence was cogent, well presented and brief.

Father Murphy was more bellicose and long winded. Mrs Doherty, under a severe cross examination reminiscent of the Inquisition, gave evidence that while Eva had not attended the RC chapel, she had seen her on occasion standing at the chapel gate admiring the building. It seems, Mrs Doherty told Father Murphy and the gathered, that Eva's look was like that of a person who desired with all her heart and soul to enter the chapel but was banned by convention. Mrs Doherty it seems, had previously told her sister Mary Ennis (nee Doherty), that Eva's look reminded her of their own sister Brenda's look, the night she told the gathered family she had a vocation and wished to become a nun. There was much murmuring among the gathered. A few blessed themselves. It was not clear when she had told her sister this version of events but the telling under oath was sufficient. Though, it was probably the implicit threat of excommunication inherent in Father Murphy's voice that played on her mind.

The Rosary Beads were of course the key, while her alignment was like icing on the cake, but the latter orientation was brought into dispute in later Court proceedings. For those Court hearing, plans of the house were drawn, maps of the surrounding town lands copied, surveyors hired to map coordinates. An expert on fires and the effect of heat on bodies was brought in and cross examined. He argued, it was not a voluntary alignment by Eva but one driven by the intensity of the heat. She had instinctively dragging herself away from the fire and by pure coincidence was found in the east west alignment, so hotly contested, pardon the pun. He even threw a bit of Pompeii and shriveling bodies in but that went over most people's head.

In the end, the High Court in Dublin found for the Sacred Heart and the legal bill of four hundred and sixty six pounds eighteen shillings was sent to the Reverend Gambles Bishop. Father Murphy never saw the hundred pounds, having died the previous summer. In fact, no one saw the money, as another court deemed Eva to have died intestate, that is without a Will and everything went to Mrs Singh's extended family back in India.

The road that passed the cottage's front door was more a glorified lane. My Da called it the M1, as it had a reservation of grass and weeds running up the middle, giving the impression of having two lanes. On a busy day chaos could ensue, when the post bike, Seany Jameson's TVO tractor and Hugh McGroddy's donkey Jessie and her milk cart, all tried to navigate the bend at the Hump. The Hump being named in memory of Tagdh McCrea, who came off his bike one evening at the spot. Tagdh was what we called in them days a hunch back, like your man in Notre Dame. The location, like so many others in the county, was named by association.

A few weeks before we arrived, Tom's oul faithful companion had given birth to a litter. She was called Cheddar. When he had found her, the bottom quarter of her right hind leg was badly broken. The bone piercing through the skin. The wound had gone septic. It had the smell of cheese about it he told us. They sedated her with a concoction of Poitin mixed with warm milk and chopped the rancid piece off, sealing the wound with fire. Since then, she had remained his loyal sidekick.

'She still has a bit of a wanderlust,' he said. 'There was a bit of the "whore" in her,' he'd laugh. 'Hobbling off for days on end coming back shagged in more ways than one.'

My Ma would ask him to use less colourful language, when the young ones were about but he revelled in making us laugh and her squirm in a soft joking way. The litter of pups were like cheddar cheeses, for despite their all coming from the same place, they were all different. Some had snub noses and neat ears like her, others big pointed noses with flopping ears and several types in between. He tried to foist one on my Ma but she said my Da would take a fit. Word was sent out via Conn Harkan, the postman, that Tom had pups free to good homes. There hadn't been many takers. One or two inquired about taking several but Tom refused to let them go, as the parties in question had a bad reputation for abusing animals. The fact we all knew, on the third night of our visit, he had taken four of the litter, the runts, down to the lough and drown them in a bag didn't amount to abuse. It was doing the decent thing. They couldn't all be kept. Nor could they be dumped somewhere out along the road to fend for themselves. To die of starvation or be beaten or shot to death he said, by locals fearful they would attack sheep.

The Cabinet of Curiosities was a magnet to us kids. At eighteen, some of my curiosity had worn thin. The bits that still drew my attention were, the melted bullet shell casings and the unexploded and live mortar shell. Or at least he claimed it was live. There was also the small wooden box inlaid with what he told me was mother of pearl. Mother of pearl being an iridescent layer of material that makes up the lining of many molluscs, for example pearl oysters. The workmanship was superb and the designs were of a style wholly alien to me. He told us it had been given to him as a gift but its quality and obvious value, were out of proportion to the other odd jumble of dusty and morbid curiosities, he claimed, he had been gifted or collected over the years.

The most macabre of which being two black withered human fingers. The fingers and the shells he said, had been brought back from the Second World War by the son of a neighbour. The son Cathal O'Connell, had volunteered to fight against the Nazis despite the Republic, to its eternal shame, being neutral during that war. He told me, Cathal argued some causes are bigger and take precedence over the internal internecine squabbles of home. Cathal survived the war unscathed, only to be shot dead by his own lot in the fifties, having voiced traitorous words about the local IRA and its commander. Over the years, there had always been something hollow in the tale of the fingers. Little discrepancies. Where they were found, the year, the likely donor and so on.

That summer I had stayed on beyond the usual two weeks. My Ma and the others, driven back home by Tommy via Derry for a day's shopping.

Sitting that first night with Tom, he on the right of the great fireplace puffing on his pipe, creating more smoke than the fire and me on the left. A nip of Poitin in a china teacup in my hand. One of the three china tea cups he processed.
'Poitins not like other drink,' he claimed. 'It was taken for purely medicinal purposes. It countered the cold and the raw edge of the hard Donegal weather.

Many a child wouldn't have made it to manhood were it not for being suckled with a little Poitin and warm milk,' he told me.

'What kept you on?' he asked. I was caught unawares and prevaricated some nonsense. Looking at me, his large hazel eyes reflecting the flames, he smiled one of those corner of the mouth smiles, the pipe clenched in his teeth rising perceptibly. I sat in contemplation.

'It's this land son,' he proffered. 'It's the smells, the firmness beneath your feet, the Corncrake crying on the far side of the lough, an early morning mist lying weightless on the fauna. A cleanliness to the air, like it was turning your lungs inside out.'

He was right. It was the land. I had been in these parts on only three or four previous occasion but on each, imperceptibly, I had been transfused. The green life blood of the county was mingled. I hadn't quite gone native but I was teetering. The previous morning, I had sat on the rough stone boundary wall that marked his meagre plot. Built from the stones, that year on year oozed up from the earth, to lie like creamy lumps of potato in brown stew. The unfolding landscape sown together with hard stone stitching. Like one of those Women's Institute patchwork quilts. Except the women were all tipsy on sherry and gin. Their fingers erratic and manic. Like the stitching on Frankenstein's monster. But this was no ugly monster. Yes it was hard and at times a brutal place. Where eking a living, never mind a livelihood, could break the hardest man. It was no land of milk and honey. The landscape peppered with empty houses paid testament to that fact.

There was something primeval about it. It appealed to the ape in me. The ape now on his heels. Standing. Homo erectus. Able to look out over the land. To see a horizon. Many had wondered what was beyond and had gone but the place remained in them, part of them, bone and sinew, hard and taut. Standing in New York canyons of steel and brick. Straining to see the sky. Beneath their feet the vibration of civilisation in inverted comas. Tarmac and concrete, a lifeless smear between them and the earth. Natural components bastardised and spread to seal down and seal in Mother Earth. The perfumed scent of gasoline on their noses. Streets peppered with little patches of green.

Where they could sit on park benches and pretend that it was home.

But when it rained in those other places, they only thought of Donegal and their true home.

'I don't know,' I replied. 'It's like somethings taking hold of me. When I go to lift my feet and walk, it's as if each foot weights ten stone. Like I have those big boots on worn by Aldrin and Armstrong on the moon.

'I was born wearing heavy boots,' he rejoined. 'And the wind Tom, it whispers to me.' 'Love me and I will love you back,' it says. 'Not with blind obedience, not with soft tones and oaths of fidelity but with a hard love. A love that anchors you, swaddles you, breast feeds you, pays a price for you.'

'Like a mothers love,' he offered.
It hurts me to think of it. What do I give it in return? My head, my heart, my life?'

'Your soul, Martin. It wants your soul. There is love of country and love of home. When a man abroad says he misses Ireland, he means he misses home, the hearth, the piece of soil where his ancestors are rooted. I am Dunlewey first, Donegal second and Ireland third. And you Martin, what are you. Are you Belfast, Antrim and the wee black North?'

'I don't know, I want to be but how. My home is like a fiction, a country born of hatred and dissent,' I sighed.
I must have sounded morose.
You're catching Donegalitis,' he cackled, realising he needed to drag me out of the hole I was digging.

'You'll work it out in due course,' he added. But it was little comfort. I watched him pulling at his pipe, the smoke puffing out in little cotton balls. He reminded me of an old steam train. Strong, resilient, reliable with a purpose straight lined and certain.

The next morning I woke with weariness upon me, my bones and limbs unrested by a bad night's sleep, a creak in my neck from dozing off on a high hard pillow.

'What do you stuff in the pillows,' I asked. 'Turnip and spuds and for people I don't like stones.'

He handed me a cup of tea. You could have tarmacked the road with it. It's brownness almost black. Half a pint of milk would not have lightened it. He noticed the look on my face.

'That will put hairs on your chest like stalks of rhubarb,' he said.

His secret was to leave the large black teapot on the edge of the fire, topping it up every few hours with tea and water. It stewed away like the witches brew in Macbeth. The pile of swollen loose leaf tea leaves, every few days tipped out of the pot onto the compost heap to decompose.

'Why have you never married?' I asked, surprising myself more than him, as the question had never entered my head before.

'In these parts it's hard to meet someone. Especially someone you might want to spend the rest of your life with. Anyway, what woman would want an existence like this? Subsisting. It wouldn't be right. I don't mind the hardships, I never have. It's my penance. I have no desire for the soft things in life. If I had, I would have gone to the big smoke, Dublin or across.'

'Your penance,' I queried. The scent of a story on my nose. He had slipped up deliberately or by mistake, I am not sure.

'What would you need to be penitent about,' I asked forcing the knife in like the oyster shucker. I sipped the tea, my eyes fixed on the turf fire. Not looking up I knew he was studying me. The scented peat smoke wafted between us like a lace veil. Intangible yet real. Like the mantilla my Ma had to wear to chapel. Designed to hide the sirens face, lest like Medusa, she turned all men to stone. I knew if I looked at him, if I spoke again, he would retreat, evade me and my curiosity. Turn me to stone.

'It's a grand morning we'll take our tea outside,' he announced. 'Top me up while I fix a pipe.'

He handed me the yellowed empty cup. The inside stained brown. The ceramic surface veined with the cracks of use. The words "I Love New York" stained and tarnished like the rotting lungs of the giver, his cousin Oisin who died young, the Pennsylvania coal dust smothering him. Filling both cups, I walked out into a warm sun, the sky Madonna blue and cloudless. At the side of the cottage, a large flat stone had been manhandled to create a seat, propped up on two large rocks protruding out of the cottage wall. I sat. Errigal in the distance, loomed to remind us of our insignificance. You can climb me but I'll still be here when you are gone she said.

'The stone, the one you're sitting on was found out there,' he indicated a general direction with the nod of his head as he approached. 'My grandfather discovered it one day when cutting peat. Just lying in the bog. There was six of them in a sort of circle he told me. In them days, they had no idea of their significance. They dug two of them out. It took them nine days, on and off to manhandle this one to here.'

We sat in silence. A bee buzzing in pursuit of pollen. One of ten thousand insects busying themselves that morning in the ever turning cycle of life. The worms turning soil, ants foraging, the wasps killing aphids. Each doing its bit. The ecosystem in harmony despite man's disruptive influences.
'Do you know no Irish Martin?' he inquired, again. On each visit he would make the same inquiry. Little or none I would repeat. We don't do it in the north, I'd add as grain for his mill. Which he would happily crush. 'Sure they have no culture banning all that's Irish.'

He was a fluent speaker, his home being set in the middle of the Gaeltacht, one of only a small number of areas where Irish is spoken as a first language. I did it for a year,' I added as some form of solace for him. 'I'm afraid it doesn't have much relevance in the province anymore,' I had said foolishly on one occasion. He looked at me aghast.

'It will one day, mark my words it will one day. A country without its own language, its mother tongue, is a country without a story. A country needs eyes to see its future. It needs ears to hear its people. But more than that it needs a language, as a common voice, so its people can converse as one. A voice made from its history. Taken from its hills, fields and rivers. Language born out of the earth that forms it, the seas that surround it, the sky that roofs it. Not language carried from another place and imposed. How can I truly express how I feel, what I believe, using another man's words.'

He was on a quiet rant. 'You just did,' I replied.
'It's not the same,' he stumbled, 'you heard it in English but you would have felt it in Irish.'
I sipped my tea as he looked at me with the corner of his left eye.

'Is fearr Gaeilge bhriste na Bearla cliste,' I said. 'You dirty devil I'm impressed.'

'It's the Da, he's rubbing off on me,' I retorted. 'There's hope for you yet.'

I basked in his praise.
'Do you know why it's called the Poisoned Glen,' he asked.

'No,' I replied. Which was a white lie, my Da having informed me of its history years previous. The glen rests at the heel of Errigal and is renowned for its beauty. It is said the glen was called the Heavenly Glen.

The story is its name was mistranslated from the Irish to English.

The Irish for heaven being neamh and poison being neimhe.

'You've been coming here for years and you don't know. I despair. Youth is wasted on the young.' I said nothing, thinking he would take a moment or two to savour the telling. But he didn't mentioned it more.

'There was someone,' he almost whispered it. 'A long time in the past.' I thought he was whispering in case he would be overheard, though it was unlikely given the nearest neighbour was half a mile away. He sipped at the tea. He was not a man to be hurried. He had the islander's mentality.

'It would never have worked,' he added, more to reassure himself the actual outcome was the natural one. Preordained.

'And why was that Tom?' I asked in the most grown up and sympathetic tone I could muster. 'She wasn't a local if you know what I mean. She was the other side. Nothing would have come of it.'

'Eva.'
'Why do you mention her?'
'The Rosary Beads, in the little wooden box. And the cuttings from the newspapers. The ones about the fire and the disappearance.'

'You were prying.' He didn't say it in an angry way but the word prying had its own connotation. 'I was curious,' I replied, a little guiltily. 'It's a Cabinet of Curiosities. What would you expect but for the young to be curious about its contents.'

'I suppose,' is all he said. I waited.
'You can tell me if you want,' I ventured nonchalantly, the fingers on my left hand crossed.

'Look it wasn't anything serious. I had a notion. She was nearly the same age. I met her when I was working at the Big House. I worked in the stable. Mucking out, grooming, and polishing saddles and bridles. Every Tuesday and Friday morning she would ride out with Mr Gregory, the estate manager. The mother had never sat on a horse and the Maharaja, as we called the Major General, was usually to drunk or too angry or too lazy to join her. He was a hateful man, God forgive me. He brought back from India, in concentrated form, the English colonial disease. We were peasants. If he hadn't fallen off his horse and broke his neck during a local hunt, he'd have been shot to death by half a dozen of the more republican minded around here.' He drew breath.

'She was seventeen like myself. A dusty beauty. Her skin like silk, with a honey hue. Tall for her age with strong broad shoulders. Her hair was the mothers, dark, luscious, thick. But her eyes were his blue, pool like.'

I said nothing. He was no longer with me, he was back there, back in the twenties with the blushing heart of a young man, smitten. He was talking not to me but to himself. His tone, that of the broken hearted. I held my breath in case my breathing disturbed the moment. It was clear he had not spoken to anyone about her or his feelings like this before. His words, were new born babies, conceived in the past and now finally delivered. I don't suggest for one moment that I felt tears in his words. He was old school. A man of rock.

Emotionless, god forbid he be seen as weak. He was a human Errigal. Battered and bruised by life's elements. Ragged round the edges but stoic.

'You were in love,' I offered, knowing well the longing of the loss.

'I suppose I was,' he replied with a half-smile. 'The folly of youth.'

'The fate of youth,' I retorted. It was our badge of honour. Battered and grieving. We put the plasters on our seeping wounds and soldiered on.

'We went to the house the night before the fire. My father, Oisin and one or two others. We had heard the rumours. My father offered to move valuables from the house, though it was clear a lot of items had been removed. We later discovered they had been sold to help the needy in the parish. She was having none of it. But she asked that one item be taken out.'

'The Cabinet of Curiosities,' I pre-empted him.
'It was her mothers. Left there by her at Eva's request, as a remembrance. We loaded it up on the milk cart and wheeled it down here, wrapped in sheets. And there it has remained.
The next night a unit of volunteers from further south arrived. They set fire to the house.'

'They knew she was in it,' I asked.
'They told her to leave, she refused. They killed her, a young woman protecting her home. He said it was an accident. The gun went off as they were dragging her out. He swore to me it was an accident. They left her where she fell. Alive. They ran like cowards.'
'Who was he?'
'It doesn't matter who he was.'

I asked because there was another paper clipping in the cabinet. Local Volunteer Disappears was the headline. It was dated three months after the fire. The story was about the strange disappearance of a Phelim Mularkey. He was eighteen and had been missing four weeks when the story was published. The paper named him as one of the arsonists. It speculated he had left the country to avoid arrest.

'What happened to him? Did he go on the run as they say?'
He ran alright. But not far.'
And then he said it. There was no emotion. His words came out even, the tone level.
'I cut them off.' I waited.
'I cut them off. The offending fingers. His fingers. They pulled the trigger.'

'The ones in the cabinet,' I said turning to face him.
'I cut them off before I killed him.'
Before I killed him. Little words. They fell to earth. Pit patting like the first raindrops of an almighty shower.
'The Rosary Beads where did they come from?' I asked, fighting to modulate a calm tone.

'That was me. I ran to the house. It was an inferno. She was lying in the front portico. There was no sign of blood, I thought she had fainted or had been knocked unconscious. The heat was unbearable. I dragged her out to the steps. It was only then I noticed the hole and blood stain. The bullet had gone in just below her left breast. The doctors examining her later said the bullet didn't exit having struck a bone. She had bled internally. I don't know why I did it but I put the Rosary around her neck. Later, I convinced myself it was a rational decision to ensure a Christian burial.' 'A Catholic one you mean.'

'The Rosary Beads, how come you still have them.'
'I stole them back, when they left her in the chapel over night. They had served their purpose.'
'And the famous alignment,'

'Pure chance. I laid her across the bottom step which were themselves aligned east west. I heard voices. I thought they had come back so I ran. I ran like a coward. People assumed she had crawled out of the house. I told no one.'

'Where is he?' 'Who?'
'Phelim.'
'Out there. In the bog. They will find him in a thousand years and think he is one of those sacrificed ancient Celts. The fingers will really screw their theories up,' he said, tossing the tea leaves on the small flower bed that ran down the side wall of the cottage.

'More tea?'

The Heron, the Watch and the Cupboard

It was the summer of seventy four. I feel a song coming on. The troubles had set new landmarks in brutality. Catholics and Protestants, Christians one and all, killing each other tit for tat. My Grandad said, if the place was full of gold and silver mines and swimming in oil, he might have understood murder for greed. But the place had nothing. The Linen gone. It's once great shipyards and engineering works only skin and bones now.

It was decided by my Da we should get out of the city for a while and so with our lives packed up in our suitcases, Jem, his sister Eileen, my Ma and I, were bundled into Tommy's oul Wolseley, like war time evacuees and driven out of the metropolis to the greener pastures of County Monaghan. I had protested to no avail. Send the women and children I had suggested. We the men would stay to defend hearth and Though, my Ma would have been happy to see our hearth being removed.

I'm seventeen Da, I pleaded. It's just as easy to kill a seventeen year old as anyone else, was his angle. It's only for a week. Your Ma needs a bit of support.

It's all taking its toll on her, he argued. I relented. Having filled the boot and an oul roof rack, which Tommy had borrowed to carry my mattress wrapped in a plastic tarpaulin, we had crawled off down the street with neighbours waving us goodbye. Tommy, the one time street fighter and part time bar fly at the helm. Steering the thirty year old Wolseley, through shattered streets cast with the detritus of battle. Weaving his way through makeshift barricades. The skeletons of buses and Lorries like fossilised dinosaur.

The farmhouse, the target of our journey, was located on a little back road, sort of half way between Cootehill and Ballybay, in the County of Monaghan. Monaghan like counties Cavan and Donegal had been amputated as part of the lifesaving operation to bring peace to the island of Ireland. A device designed to give two Christian people's room to live and prosper. Or at the very least, to stop them from slaughtering each other. The operation being a failure in part. The South limped on and made a slow recovery. But it was like the amputee, convinced they can still feel the missing limb. The North at first, appeared robust but there was an underlying malignancy. The artificial division, was part of the plan brought back by Mick Collins in 1921, too bring to an end the old English Irish conflict, that had left Ireland bloodied and battered for nearly six hundred years. A bandage on a seeping, diseased wound.

A protracted conflict of interests the English just didn't understand. What was it about the Irish, they asked themselves, that they couldn't see the benefit of infusing the superiority of the English into their blood and culture? The good will of the English upper classes, freely given, to raise the Irish from the bog of ignorance in which they wallowed. An ungrateful shower. Frustrated by our intransigence, they used the old colonial wheeze of drawing lines on maps, drawing lines through people's land and lives. With no regard for reality or the victims it would create. Just like India twenty five years later, which led to a million murders. But then they were only darkies and we were only Paddy's, Micks, an inferior race, a lesser species. We were all Barbarians when the English came and civilised us. Sure didn't they give us the common law and the common language? The language of commerce, erudition and gentility. Of Shakespeare, Chaucer and the St James Bible. Their civil service, though there was nothing civil about them if you were Irish.

But we got our own back on them. The three counties of Ulster snaffled from them and ethnically cleansed. The Anglo Irish Protestant, incrementally transported with good riddance back home or to their wee corner in the North. The little clean, tidy, demure churches standing in the three stolen counties as testimony to there being and going. Only their dead lying soft in Irish soil, left to mark remembrance. Smyth, Poots, Elliot and Greyling. And so what if we had to sacrifice some of our own in the six counties. If they want to stay with the Protestants in the North let them. What a shambles it all turned out to be.

We crossed the border at Tyholland, having passed through the large army checkpoint in Middletown. Stopping at the two border posts, we looked like refugees with all our worldly possessions strapped in and onto the car. We weren't the first. Stopping at the Irish post, Tommy went into the office with the customs officer, emerging ten minutes later with a purple triangle of paper, which he had to display on the front window of the car. There wasn't a lot of traffic. A few Lorries were parked up in a siding, their drivers with greasy spoon bacon and egg bellies, standing in a group puffing on fags, waited for clearance, so they could continue their journey.

Jem had driven me to distraction with his constant questioning, as to whether we were there yet. My Ma and Tommy seemed oblivious to him, as they talked incessantly through the whole journey. Jem's sister Eileen, the opposite, who never spoke. She was fourteen. A pretty girl with short dark hair and steel blue eyes. Her figure not yet formed giving her quite a boyish look. She read for most of the journey, undisturbed by Jem's whining and constant fidgeting. He was a hive of activity. The hair on his head wild and unkempt, the eyes lively and darting. He seemed to have little control over his mouth or his movements. I imagined he would one day burn out like an overused AA battery but twenty years on he would be the same, bursting with life, asking the wrong question at the wrong time, pointing out the failings of the world around him, thrusting headlong. All of us expecting him to come a cropper. Failed businesses, failed marriage, failed parenthood, carnage left in his wake and he still oblivious. Yet it was none of that.

We made a rest stop in Monaghan at the Westenra Arms Hotel, which was a posh watering hole in the centre of the town. We're on holiday, lets spoil ourselves Tommy had said. Eileen stole a bar of soap from the ladies toilet. Jem said, she was a nymphomaniac but Tommy said it was kleptomaniac, which sounded worse. Monaghan town in them days was the county's big smoke. A solid sort of town, built around an ancient central green, which at that stage had been tarmacked but still had a grand feel to it. The Main Street and "Diamond" were well provisioned with quality shops. Shoes and men's clothing being prominent. A substantial sandstone neo classical train station stood at the northern end of town, while a similar style building housed a library. A local livestock market adjoined the station. The station was closed in 1959.

A herd of young bulls was being driven through the town, past the Alma Monument, as we drove out. We pulled in to allow their passage. Doe eyed and multi coloured they clattered through the Diamond, one or two leaving deposits through fear or defiance as they went. Squeezing passed the Wolseley, one stopped to look in on us, pushing his nose up against the rear side window leaving a smear of his breath on the glass.

'Ah they are so cute,' said Eileen. 'Ah they are so tasty,' said Tommy.

We all laughed, bar Eileen, who now did silent plus huff for the remainder of the journey.

We took the Rockcorry Road, its twists and turns like a corkscrew. The land wasn't the best, having a reputation of being heavy soiled and damp. Many of the fields were blanketed with reed like grass, pretty much inedible to all forms of livestock. No good to beast or man I heard said. But the sun was out and the fields shimmered a multiplicity of green under its gaze, though perhaps not quite forty shades. We wound down the windows, the wind rushing through the car as we sped along at twenty eight miles an hour. My Ma tied her hair up with a polka dot ribbon she pulled from her hand bag. To stop it turning into a haystack she said. She looked like Debra Kerr from the back. Jem on occasion stuck his head out the window, being chastised on each event about the dangers of flying objects and telegraph poles. Rather than taking the back road to the lough at Muney we stayed on the road to Cootehill.

Tommy said he would tell us later about the headless horseman, The Dullahan On our right we passed the walls of the Dartry Estate, which once had one thousand acres of lakes within its boundaries. While on the left stood The Dawson Monument. Given the heat of the day, Tommy said he would treat us to an ice cream at Mary Buzzers.

Cootehill, once a prosperous linen town, was across the county border in Cavan. It had a broad single main street called Market Street, at the end of which stood the Church of Ireland, the Post Office, the entrance to the Belmont Estate, the Court House and the White Horse Hotel all of which seem to make the street top heavy. The town was named in honour of the marriage of Thomas Coote, a Cromwellian Colonel and Francis Hill, one of the Hills of Hillsborough, a landed family from County Down. Along the length of the street there were twenty pubs. In a former life Tommy would have been in his element. At this stage, he had been on and off sober nearly two years. He never spoke of the catalyst that brought him to semi sobriety and we never asked.

My Ma wandered down the street, telling Tommy he could pick her up at the far end of town. We ate our ice creams on the old bench outside Mary Buzzers shop, while Tommy conversed with a couple of locals. At that time, it was suggested the oldest known humans came out of Ethiopia 200,000 years previous. I am not convinced, for standing looking at these men, they looked older than the land that bore their weight. Father and son their mannerisms mirror images. The stance. A hand in the left pocket tucked in under the jacket flap. Their feet boot clad, one straight, the other pointing slightly in. Hen toed my Granny called it. Their exposed right hands thick and calloused. Checked Paddy caps at a jaunty twenty five degrees. Two days stubble like miniature pins and as sharp. But the demeanour was that of the friend. There was nothing negative in the body language. They stood grown from the soil, though on the tarmac of the street they seemed a little out of place.

'Who's these fine lookin Gasuns,' asked the local. 'These are Johnnie Connolly's niece and nephews,' Tommy said, not seeking to differentiate us. 'Up for a week's holiday.' 'Connolly's at the lough,' questioned the younger man.
'The same,' confirmed Tommy.
'A fine man, a good family,' declared the father. 'Tell them Jim O'Grady was asking after them.' Shaking Tommy's hand, he and his fellow traveller made their way down the street thirty yards, before turning into the first pub.

Can we walk down the street after Ma, I asked? Tommy nodded his agreement.

'Just keep an eye on Jem,' he called. Jem scowled back. Being a warm day some of the shops, the butchers and grocers had awning wound out to shade their window display, others had dark yellow tinted plastic shades pulled down on the inside of the window.

'What's them for,' asked Jem?

'So the things in the window won't fade in the sunlight,' replied Eileen.

Jem was unimpressed. We wandered on. There weren't a lot of cars about. The odd delivery van was parked up. A Bolands bread van was parked outside a shop called Farrells. The back open, the driver was pulling large sliding trays in and out with a long hooked pole. We stopped to stare. Each tray was festoon with breads of all shapes and sizes, most unwrapped. One tray had various pastries, Apple Turnovers, Paris Buns, Pink Coconut Squares. My mouth watered. Eileen and I dragged Jem away under protest, as he attempted to steal a Paris Bun.

Outside a grocery store we stopped to admire the multi coloured display of vegetable. Mr Mellor would have been in his element, I thought. Jem said yuck. Behind us we heard the old Wolseley's horn. Looking at her laden with our worldly possessions, in particular my mattress, I thought of the story The Grapes of Wrath, parts of which my Da had read to me the previous summer.

We climbed aboard and a hundred yards on picked up my Ma. Who now carried a small plain brown paper bag?

'What's that,' asked Jem. 'Is it buns?'

No is all she said. We drove out of town past the Catholic chapel built in 1927 now dominating the town. Further on we skirted the livestock mart and abandoned railway station. By the 1950's the vast majority of railway lines were torn up as cars and road transport began to dominate. At one time Ireland had 3,500 miles of railway lines. The lines crisscrossing the country, north to south, east to west, like sutures stitching the country together. My Da had once described the lines more physically as its arteries and veins. Pumping the life blood of goods and people around the country. Orderly and structured the English sought to impose their time and certainty on us. The running of the railways was like a microcosm of the old English Irish struggle. They seeking to run on time, us to run in time. They would never understand us and in ignorance and arrogance exasperated the problem. We were never a people of urgency. Not quite the Spanish Manjana, Manjana, we fell somewhere in between. Between two stools you might say.

We kept left at the Jet petrol station, turning left again at Brady's and a hundred yards on, right onto the road to Latton. More a lane than a road it twisted and yawled like the Helter Skelter at Mosney. Blind corners were taken at ten miles an hour. The grass verges uncut were verdant. Buttercups, Daisies, Red Clover and other wild flowers vied for space and attention. Lined up like the crowds in Finaghy, waiting with bated breath, to see the Queen as she passed by on a royal visit. They waved at us, swaying in admiration as we passed them. Jem his hand, arm, shoulder and head slung out the window, oblivious to Tommy's remonstrations, shook hands with the crowd, who gently excited by our passing smiled and cheered our progress.

A mile or so on we passed a small slightly dilapidated cottage, the whitewash dulled by the elements. At the door sat Annie McGinn. Her black dress, shawl and small stature giving her a Queen Victoria appearance. If it wasn't for the long clay pipe she puffed on, she'd have been her dead ringer. Though, it wouldn't have surprise me, if Victoria, on her days off had supped on a secret pipe, probably an opium one. We waved our passing.

'Not far now,' announced Tommy.
'About time,' whined Jem. Eileen sighed. Her breath carrying the silent words of adolescent indignation and indifference. The lough came into view on the right. There she is, I said the quiver of excitement on my lips. Why did I speak of this body of water as she? What was it about this place that held such a fascination it made me blush like the shy boy?

An elixir of love seemed to snake through me, my blood a little different, fired up. Like those early days embarrassed at my thoughts, hardness down below. I put my hands on my lap. I need help I thought. Jem broke my chain.

'Can we go in the boat,' he demanded with menace. 'Let's get there first. We need to get ourselves sorted out. Unpack. You and Martin need to sort the mattress out. You are in the room over the storehouse,' explained my Ma.

'Storehouse awh,' groaned Jem.
Awh is right I thought a week in one room with Jem. I'll be done for manslaughter before the week is out. My only consolation being the room looked directly over the lough. With murder on my mind we drew up at the house. Tommy, turning the Wolseley between the cream and red piers into the front yard.

The house, of two storeys, was built of stone with a fine heavy slate roof. It sat back from the road, the yard and wall protecting it from passing traffic. All ten vehicles a day. Mainly tractors. The little grey transverse oil tractors produced by Ferguson. Little work horses simple and reliable. On the left, stood a set of outhouses where various types of livestock were housed. To the right, the long storehouse with a corrugated roof, housed bits of machinery, tools and Uncle Johnnies black Ford Zephyr Mk IV. A little red Massey Ferguson tractor was parked up on the right, between house and storehouse, where a set of doors punctuated its long wall. In later years, a garage was built along the front of the yard giving the place the feel of an Italianate cortile.

Across the road was the lough. Baraghy Lough is a glorious expanse of fresh water teeming with wildlife. It is unusual in that it straddles the county borders, with half in Cavan and the other half in Monaghan. It is an odd shape being nipped in the middle like it is wearing one of those Victorian corsets.

On the front of the house stood a small vestibule with a single solid front door. Passing through it, a second half glass door gave admittance to the kitchen, the heart of the house. To the right, stood a large cast iron stove with an oven and hot plates. The main heating in the house. To its right, a door which led into the shop.

From the shop the upper floor could be accessed by an open wooden stair, which was more like a permanent ladder. To access the three rooms above, you had to pass through each room as there were no halls or corridors. A common feature of the vernacular Irish dwelling. The internal walls were roughly plastered and the ceilings low. Single windows in the front wall of each room gave limited light. Single double flex cable lights hung from the ceiling giving meagre illumination to the rooms at night. Electricity being a 1960's afterthought. Even in the Seventies the toilet was outside. A bath would be had, in front of the cast iron range, in a large galvanised mobile basin, hung up in the storehouse until required.

Up until the late Fifties water was drawn in buckets from the lough and heated on the cast iron range. The loughs water clean and purely filtered through nature. In later years, it would become impregnated with the residues of fertilisers, sprayed on the undulating boundary fields and leached down by natural processes. The banks of Cattails emboldened by the fertilisers spreading outwards, reducing the waters footprint. The rampant Duckweed, choking the small streams that flowed from numerous little valley surrounding the gentle water filled depression.

I recalled from earlier visits, the fine old four man boat, lying arse up on a tiny shoreline etched by the soft lapping of the waves created by the prevailing wind. Forbidden to us, in case we would meet the same fate, as oul Patsy Jim Pat's mad uncle Padraig. On a night of fierce storms he boarded the boat, no one knew why, and rowed himself out into the lough. We heard Patsy calling out like a man demented, said my uncle Johnnie. It was all we could do to drag him out of the water. Padraig had rowed out about seventy five yards. The storm was rough but visibility was fine. He just stopped rowing and sat there, the boat bobbing and turning like it was dancing. Padraig quietly humming to himself. Then a gentle mist enveloped him. Pulled round him by God to spare us seeing the tragedy of his going. The humming stopped. There was no splash, no cry for help. Just the cry of a Heron, as it raised itself with effort from the lough. In its cry we heard the fine voice of his parting. He had been a great chanter in his day. A talented storyteller. A repository of the parish's history. There wasn't a place or family for twenty mile around he hadn't got a story or tale to tell about them.

Patsy had looked after him the twenty years prior. The two inseparable. Patsy's wife Mary having died in childbirth with their first. The two would be seen on alternate market days in Cootehill and Ballybay parking up the TVO at Carneys or Lynch's pub. Having dined on boiled cabbage and spuds served in their jackets, butter dripping, washed down with a pint or two of porter they would stroll to the mart. Their journey punctuated with constant stops to shake hands, pass salutations. The conversations always the same, the weather, the price of livestock, word of emigrants and those fecking wide boys up in the big smoke, ruining the country. In later years, Patsy would tie the uncle to the TVO's dickie seat to stop him jumping off while in motion. On Sunday's the two, dressed like dummies out of Clearys window, would roll up to Latton chapel for mass. Cold shaved and cat licked spotless save their hands. Their fingers like black puddings. Hard, calloused, impregnated with the earths stain. A lifetime grubbing in the soil.

Their best suits, the same twenty years past. Three pieces, white shirt, the collar frayed, dark tie tightly knotted. Patsy's black brogues, polished thin uppers, the sole and heel in their third generation. Padraig with heavy black working boots, forerunners of Doc Martens. Taking a pew at the back near the side door, so they could slip out fast at the end for a fag. Gathered with clones they talked the latest news and gathered updates on Cathal's demise or Eddy's heifers, the cost of vets and hay. The travails of the local GAA team and the loss of a fine footballer, young Donal Murdoch to education in the big smoke, Dublin's gain.

They would stay there huddled as the chapel spilled its flock through open doors, like the blood of Christ spilled from his open wounds. To those leaving greetings, nods of recognition, reminders to call in the next time they were passing. Offers of work, offers of assistance. A community. Father Malachy stopping for a few moments to draw smoke with them. His fag crumpled, tip less, bobbing on the corner of his mouth as he greeted all as one. His parting shot to remind them about confessions. His lilting Limerick goodbye.

These were the last of the true landed country men. Sons of the soil. Men who knew their world intimately. The turning of the season, the turning of the rill, the turning of the weather, the turning of the bones to put another on top. They could smell life.

They knew its true price. Having grown up when hand to mouth meant just that. They enjoyed the bounty of the earth they stood on, relative to how much they had and how good it was. Much of it boggy and water logged sustaining a few sheep or a milking cow. As children they had worked it like the adults, the potato rills waiting for them on return from school. Walking three mile at five in the morning to gather up the dairy cows. Following them home and back their udders swollen like Scotch bagpipes. Rhythmically swaying between their back legs, high boned women, black and white and earth red.

Still there an old monochrome photo taking pride of place on the good room wall. Taken in late November, 1930 at Derrygooney School. Pupils and teachers, in various states of interest and fear, look back at the taker. The poor grainy black and white finish making Victorian urchins of them.

Their clothes hand me downs. Some made up from old pieces, odds and sods sown by spinster aunts, talented mothers. The fashion designers of their day. Even the shoes, passed down as they were outgrown. Half of them shoeless, standing barefoot on the cold winter ground.

Each one could be named, their life's journey narrated for us by Johnnie. Kevin Lynch to the big smoke for bar work, Barney McGowan to the states, followed by his brother and sister two year later. Never to return home again. The last letter coming in 1952. Margaret and Paddy Connolly fourteen and fifteen respectively, sent to friends in New York who never turned up to collect them. The two children ending up in care. But didn't they get a great education, didn't they live the American Dream. And at the back Blackie McKenna who died young coughing up blood in agony. And Mary Blake, who's six all came back from America to carry her to Latton. Carneys horse drawn hearse, decked in black plumes, drawing her up the road in one of the finest funerals the county ever seem. The money tripping them.

On the counting, thirty two out of forty five gone; down, across, over, to find livelihoods, love, and loss in foreign parts. The Irish diaspora, building towns, railways and roads, populating the world. Like red blood cells pumping, replicating, carrying life's oxygen to the body earth. Mingling and spilling it in equal measure, in the new world and on the shores of other foreign parts. Some in pursuit of adventure, others a better life, some in the belief they were dying for a worthy cause. Irish blood, bone, muscle and sinew strained and drained to build a better world. People from a little island, little town lands and little towns. Small holders, leaving small holdings whose small feet made giant foot prints.

I recall being told, how Johnnie strapped Blackie's coffin to the roof of his funeral coloured Ford and drove him over the snow deep lanes to the main road, where Carney's men waited black and morbid. Like Black Widow spiders taking their prey back to the lair. There among the jars, lineaments and rags they would work their dark magic. Turning Blackie's cancer ravaged corpse into a human once again. Stuffing old newspaper in his trouser legs and arms to give him flesh and something to read on his journey, said Kevin Carney.

Especially, the sports pages from The Anglo Celt, as he was a great GAA man. A fine county footballer and hurler. His senior hurling medals put in the box with him. Half the county turning out to see him on his way. A spread of sandwiches and soup put on at the White Horse Hotel, through donations from home and abroad. His brother Francis, well to do in Chicago but too ill to travel home. He would go shortly after him, buried four thousand miles apart.

Tommy's car just about coming to a halt, Jem climbed out through the window. Half way out Eileen pulled the door handle, the door swinging out with Jem caught in no man's land. 'Ejit,' snapped Tommy more concerned for the antiquity of the car than Jem's fate. Which involved the remainder of him falling out the window on to the concrete yard. Unperturbed, he bounced up like a rubber ball and headed for the house. Eileen sat on.

'Out,' hissed the Ma, 'I've enough on my plate without you acting the princess. We are here for a week's peace and relaxation. And you Martin, keep control of him, he's like something let loose.'

So much for my week of peace and relaxation. Eileen smirked, sliding herself out the other car door, book under arm her white Patent shoes and bobby socks, picking their way through some better left unnamed deposits in the yard. My Ma followed her.

Tommy and I were left in the yard. My sympathies is all he said patting me on the back. I am convinced I saw the corners of his mouth turn up in an almost imperceptible smile.

Man handling the mattress, we deposited it on the first floor along with my case and Jem's.

'It's a grand view, beats the bakery wall hands down,' offered Tommy as consolation while standing at the window, a little flushed, hands in pocket. 'The first time I came here was fifteen year ago, July I think,' he added, 'nothing has changed yet everything has changed. Your Da and I came on the bus to Monaghan.'

So this is where he was, I thought.
'Johnnie picked us up in a big car. I'm not sure what it was. It had runner boards on the side. He loves his cars, loves the road. He'd be gone at the drop of a hat. Word would come such and such needs transport and he'd be off.'

'We were the worse for wear, we sort of got waylaid in Monaghan town. I slept the whole way. Johnnie said he couldn't hear himself over my snoring. We stayed five or six days in this very room. He drove us back to Belfast on the 11th of July and stayed to watch the Twelfth parades. We stood on the railway bridge at Finaghy and watched the Orangemen marching to the Ten Acres. Could you imagine us doing that now? Your Da, Charlie and me with Johnnie and a neighbour of his. I don't recall his name. Enjoying the July sun. God smiling down on the Orangemen as they made hay while the sun shone. And us doing a wee jig, as some shower of bigoted bastards from Glasgow or somewhere else in that god forsaken land called Scotland, marched by beating their drums like they were beating papist heads.'

'We'd be throwing stones at them now,' I offered. 'And more,' rasped Tommy. 'We better get the rest out of the car. If Jem gives you any trouble give him a good slap. He's use to it. His fathers a rough man.'

'I'll survive him. It's Eileen I'm worried about. A look from her and I want to wither up and die.'

'Wee girls. It's her hormones, they're all up the left at her age or so I am reliably told by your Da.' 'And he'd know,' I asked and stated at the same time. 'Well he'd know more than me. Being a bookworm and all,' concluded Tommy.

Taking one last look out the window he turned and trundled down the wooden stair. I followed. We manoeuvred the last of the luggage into the farmhouse, calling greetings to Aunt May as we entered. There's tea and sandwiches here she replied. Having deposited our load, we sat ourselves down at the kitchen table facing the blackened cast iron range.

My Ma was at the sink.
'Where are they all,' asked Tommy.
'Sean is over in the storehouse. Larry Mullins there doing some work on the tractor. Eileen's in the good room with Rosemary. Seamus and Eamon are at the top field, hanging a gate,' May rattled off.

'And Uncle Johnnie,' I enquired. 'He's over on the Rock.'

The Rock was just that. Situate at the Monaghan end of the lough, it gave a great vantage point to see the whole of the lough and its surrounds. Of little other use it was home to Gorse and Brambles. The two voracious invaders imbibing their way into the land through snaking networks of grubbing roots. The former, useless bar the beauty of its colour. The latter, graciously giving something back in wild fruit.

I helped myself to a cheese and ham sandwich. 'The place will be rammed tonight,' I mumbled through a mouthful of macerated sandwich. 'Seamus and

Eamon are going to spend a few nights over at Clerkin's to ease the pressure,' announced the Ma.

'No need for that,' I offered, 'they can bunk in with me and Jem. Where is he by the way?'

'He stuffed two sandwiches in his pocket, said he was going to the storehouse,' replied my Ma. 'Is the boat tied up,' asked Tommy.

'Well tied up he'll be going nowhere in it.
Himself says he'll take you out Sunday after mass for a spot of fishing,' confirmed May.

'It's hot for the oul fish, they'll all be hiding away in them reeds,' advised Tommy who knew more about quantum physics than he did about fishing, him been city born, bred and bound.
'Can we go out some night to see the bats,' I asked.
'Let's get settled in, then we can sort out who's doing what and when,' snapped my Ma.

Surreptitiously, I eyed the Victoria sponge cake resting on the windowsill, it layered with fresh cream and Mays homemade jam.

'That's a lovely looking cake,' I ventured.
'And it tastes lovely too,' replied Aunt May, 'Will you have a slice Tommy before you hit the road?'
'Don't mind if I do. Not too big a slice now as there's a lot of hungry gobs eyeing it.' He winked at me.

'I'll take a small slice to,' I said, a little bit of pleading added in for good effect.

'You'll spoil your dinner,' protested my Ma. Ignoring her May cut two slices. Tommy's was twice the size of mine. We scoffed them.

Tommy left around five, helping us before his going to put another mattress in the storeroom for Seamus and Eamon. Seamus, sixteen was a rascal of a lad. His head adorned with blonde curls like Alexander of Macedonia. Always smiling, his demeanour always active. Eamon quieter, more studious was dark haired and dark eyed. They returned from the top field around six, ten hours of work already in them. There was no rest for the wicked and the farmer, my Da had told me.

Sean, older than us all had come in earlier, degreased his hands, downed his tea and left for another job. Ever on the go he had inherited Uncle Johnnie's wanderlust. He was Johnnies mini me. Thoughts, deeds, actions just in a younger version.

Rosemary had left with Eileen half an hour earlier to bring the cows in for milking. Eileen decked out in a pair of May's old wellie boots. They leak a bit but sure you'll come to no harm May had assured her.

Sometime after six Johnnie arrived in. A solid man, average height, soft spoken, his complexion Costa del Sol, greeted us Gasuns like long lost sons. Jem half lifted, was dragged by my Ma from the top seat and placed on a stool by the range. The King had returned. Under Irish law, primogeniture, the oldest got the land and all that went with it. He was a benevolent King given the times they were. Ireland was, for all her cheeky Irish charm, a hard mistress. Her beauty was green grass deep.

'We have you for a week, well we'll put you to good use,' cooed Johnnie 'Eamon and Seamus are staying with us,' I said. 'That's good,' I saw the two look at their ma who nodded clandestinely. It struck me, that maybe I had been too hasty in making the sharing offer.

Maybe, a few days at Clerkin's would have been a holiday for them.

'More hands make light work,' pronounced Johnnie.

'How many Brits does it take to change a light bulb,' interjected Jem. 'Six hundred,' he continued without waiting our reply, 'one to hold the bulb and five hundred and ninety to turn the room.' We all laughter. 'What about the other nine?' asked Eamon. Jem looked confused.

'They were killed when the ceiling fell on them,' said Seamus.

Encouraged by the adults, we kicked around the front yard with Seamus until the cows arrived. Doddering nonchalantly into the milking parlour their udders bulging, they took up their positions like professionals. We watched as Seamus and

Johnnie placed the suction cups on each teat. The cows shaking their heads and swishing their tails in anticipation of relief.

'How many cows do you have,' enquired Jem. 'Thirty six,' replied Seamus. Jem didn't seem impressed.

'Did you get lost,' asked Johnnie when the girls appeared fifteen minutes later.

'I was showing Eileen the orchard. She had never seen one,' replied Rosemary.

'The limitations of city life,' he retorted.

I sat on a metal rail, watching the white elixir of life being pumped through the glass jars into the stainless steel tanks. The tanks, made to varying sizes, were mini tankers on two wheels. They would be hitched to the back of tractors or cars and trailed to the local cooperative milk processing plant. In some parts of the county Johnnie said milk churns were still being used to deliver milk. Churns would be filled and left in covered areas at the farm gate for collection. The original churns holding ten to seventeen gallons. Some milk would be retained for drinking, making butter milk and cheese. Over the next week, I would no doubt hear the woes of the dairy farmer. The fluctuating price of dairy cattle and other livestock prices read out from the Farmers Journal and the Anglo Celt.

At around six on Friday we heard the local death notices announced on the radio. One of Johnnies neighbours, Packy McEntee, had passed on the previous evening. God rest his soul. I asked to tag along with Johnnie and May that evening when paying their respects. The house was a hive of activity. It seemed like half the county had turned up. Outside on the street men stood in groups, fags and pipes burning. They acknowledged our arrival with clear affection. I was introduced as a fine young Gasun up from Belfast, shaking a baker's dozen of hard hands before entering the house.

Inside some women sat busy in small talk, others serving tea. On the mantelpiece stood a large black clock, its hands stopped at 10.35, the time Packy parted this world on his journey to a better place. All were certain he was going up, given he was a pious and decent man, who never had an ill word for anyone. On the back wall of the good room, the mirror was covered with a black cloth.

The same cloth used when his own father and mother passed away some twenty and thirty years earlier.

I was offered and accepted some sweet tea and a sandwich. Ham and cheese. His own ham I was told, cured on the farm to a recipe a hundred years old. It certainly didn't taste a hundred years old so I had a second. Johnnie, having paid his respects to the family, made his way out to mingle with the men in the street. To talk the talk of farmers, engrossed and preoccupied with their lot. Inside I was quizzed. What age was I? Where in Belfast did I live? The troubles, had I ever seen a bomb go off. Did I know any IRA men? Did I know that Liam O'Callaghan, across the lough, was an oul IRA man who fought in the Rising and the Civil War? Now, his son lay drunk most days, while the animals around him died in his father's fields.

There were those who remembered my Ma as a young women and enquired about her. I told them she would be at the funeral on the Monday. They seemed pleased. Another opportunity for news of the outside world first hand.

On returning to the yard, interrogated and exhausted, I found Johnnie standing, the bonnet of the Ford open like the mouth of some massive black dog. He was pointing out the finer details of the vee six engine, producing I heard him say with pride one hundred and forty horse power. The gathered impressed shuck their heads in admiration. It won't be long before there's flying cars predicted one of them.

The next morning woke me early. A cockerel somewhere, secreted behind the storehouse, was crowing about himself. He didn't impress me. Hens must be stupid, I thought, to be taken in by such a blabber mouth. Jem lay beside me oblivious, mouth open. I checked myself for bruises, Jem being the restless sort had gone six rounds with Cassius Clay before thankfully being knocked unconscious by the world champion in the fourth round. The other mattress lay empty and forlorn, the clothes a crumpled mass.

Slipping out of bed, I pulled on the same clothes and took up a perch on the windowsill. Wisps of mist lay on the lough like fine tissue paper. Two swans, old English white drifted out of the mist like ghosts, serene, silent, birds with royal assent.

One drifting a few inches behind the other. I wondered if they were a couple, him and her, Mr and Mrs. Their heads held high like they were doing deportment exercises. The nearest turned to look in my direction. Well, we are regal birds it said and turning on their submerged heels they slipped effortlessly away. I in turn slipped by Jem his face now stuffed in the pillow, his bare backside in the air, the pyjama bottoms having slipped down during his sporting travails.

I walked to the water's edge. The sticklebacks in the shallows, sensing my presence, darted away in shoals. The mist was lifting. The water was like black plate glass. Not a ripple appearing. I hunted around for flat stones to cast as skimmers. There was an art to skimming. I had memories of Eamon and another cousin, Micheal, setting world records. Or at least in those early childhood days it seemed like it.

If my memory served me well, Eamon hit seventeen skips before his stone dived to its death in the cold deep waters. Johnnie claimed the lake was a hundred metres deep in places and treacherous eddies near the Point would drag a grown man down in seconds.

Water we were taught was our nemesis, my Da having nearly drown in a small river as a child. The river passed through a local golf course, out of bounds to his ilk. He and another were searching for golf balls lost in the river, to resell them. He fell in out of his depth and was saved by the local doctor's wife, who stretching a No3 wood out to him managed to haul him to the bank. He said if he had a picture of her, his saviour, he would have kept it on his wall. My Ma said it was Gods will she had been passing at the time. My Da said it was because she'd shanked the three wood off the tee box and had come in search of her ball, a Titleist 2 he remembered, which always made good money.

I paced the line between wet and dry to where that same boat, a little worse for age, rested upside down on the shingle. I sat on the upturned bow. A Heron cried somewhere in the reeds. The air smelt of mown grass. I could now see clean across to the other side, which distance measured a good two hundred yards. A band of brown headed reeds marked the far bank, behind which fields broken into erratic portions rose up in drumlin hills. Some, still long and lush, others shaved tight like a soldiers head. Their partitions made of a mix of trees, miscellaneous shrubs, holly bushes and brambles. Partitions made in the distant past to define ownership. The mark of mans greed, his, mine, theirs, rarely hers.

My eye was drawn by a trio of ducks gliding effortless into land, not twenty metres from where I sat. Their touchdown breaking the glass momentarily, the fragmented pieces reconstructing themselves. They paddled by their mirror image swimming in unison. I was reminded of the three china ducks Aggy had hanging over her fireplace. Mallards, I believe. Each one slightly smaller than the other to create a sense of perspective. Or at least that's what my Da said. He being a knowledgeable man about perspective and the art of the Italian Renaissance, I put some store in his observation. I watched them till they disappeared around the corner of a small promontory fifty yards further along. I wished them a safe journey.

Pike had been caught in the lake with small ducks in their bellies. Voracious carnivores, Pike looked like ancient creatures. They are made for speed. Long torpedo like bodies with sharply pointed heads and a fierce mouthful of teeth make them seasoned hunters. Having been known to grow to six feet and weight up to seventy pounds. They have a reputation for being cannibalistic, sometimes feeding on their own species. One summer, Seamus only ten, caught one twenty three pounds on a kids glass fibre rod. While they look prehistoric they are quite tasty. The key is to take them alive and place them into a cistern or tank of fresh running water. Leaving them for three or four days to digest their last meals and excrete the detritus of a scavenger's appetite. In later years, fishermen from the continent came, in particular the Germans, with boats, nets and refrigerated Lorries. They netted the local lakes, unrestricted as no licenses were required. Virtually denuding the lakes of every local species of fish. Bream, roach, trout, perch and pike. The latter being a delicacy in Germany.

At the time, people were preoccupied trying to earn a crust, Johnnie told us. The fishermen brought money to the local pubs, hotels and guest houses. They were welcomed with open arms. In those days Ireland was for sale to the highest bidder. Sure County Kerry was nearly renamed Kerpen there were so many Germans buying up land there.

Rising from my makeshift seat, the bow board having driven my underpants into my nether regions, I fixed them as best I could and strode forth towards the house. As I crossed the road, a large black cat scurried out of the verge stopping momentarily to eye me. It's left front paw, brilliant white, raised almost in a clawing action. Having given me the once over, tucking its shoulders down it sped off almost crawling on its belly.

Entering I found the women gathered round the kitchen table. Plans were a foot for a baking session.

Even Eileen seemed engrossed in the scheme and gave me a smile, though it was like whiskey with too much water.

'We're making cakes and bread for the wake,' she announced.

They condescended to give me room at the table for some toast and tea. No one asked about Jem. Everyone knew mentioning his name was like saying it's too hot, which pronouncement always brought the rain.

'Where's the men,' I asked, my mouth spitting bread crumbs.

'The men have gone to their work, while boys lay in bed,' spat back Eileen. She was reverting to type. I seemed to have that effect on her.

'I would have went with them,' I offered.

'You're here on holiday,' said May coming to my defence. 'There's plenty of time for work. Don't worry, himself will find something for you to do.'

'He has to do something for his keep,' chorused my Ma who was peeling apples at the far end of the table.

'I could help you,' I suggested, taking each of them in with a fleeting glance.

'This is women's work you'd only get in our way. If you want to do something helpful go over to the top field and see if the boys need a hand. Have you boots,' enquired May. I nodded. 'Well go and get them on you. Come back here and we'll give you some tea for the lads.' I scurried out.

Climbing the stair I heard Jem talking to himself. He was having a full on discussion. Clambering over the top stair I asked who he was talking to. 'The fella that was here. Did you not pass him on the stair?'
I shook my head, as a no and to symbolise my disbelief.

'I tell you,' whined Jem, 'he was here. He said he was looking for his watch. A pocket watch he kept calling it. I said I hadn't seen it. I told him to ask someone in the house. I nearly crapped myself,' he continued. 'I woke to find him sitting on the end of the mattress. He was soaking wet. Look, look at the mattress its wet.'

He was right. At its right hand corner there was a clear damp patch. On the floor two wet fading footprints marked where the visitor must have stood. 'He walked down the stair right past you,' insisted Jem.

I thought I better play along. Maybe he had wet himself and was concocting some cover story. 'What else did he say?'

'He told me the Heron called him.' 'Who's the Heron?'

'I don't know. He said he put the watch in the cupboard. But it wasn't there. It was his father's watch handed down to him. I told him I would help him look for it. He said he would be back later.'

'You were dreaming,' I suggested half-heartedly. 'Get on you and after you have breakfast you can come with me to the top field. Don't mention anything to the others.'

'What if he has spoken to them,' he asked. 'Let's see if he did. If not say nought.'

It was clear on our entry no one had spoken to them. I shook my head to reinforce Jem's silence. 'One more for tea and toast,' I announced.
They sat him by the range, the table covered in bowls and baking paraphernalia groaned under the weight.
Four slices of toast and three cups of tea later we left port for the top field. The top field simply being the highest field on the farm.

We walked in silence, the summer heat rising. The fields around crackled with noise, filling our silence, buzzing, clicking, ticking, tweeting, digging, mooing, mowing, bleating, a cacophony of life. We heard the tractor before we saw it. Cresting the hill Eamon and Seamus came into view. We waved, they returned it.

'Should I tell them,' asked Jem. 'They might have seen him before. He might have been there when they got up,' he ventured, desperate to spill the beans.

'Let me ask them later,' I suggested. I didn't say they already think you're a bit crazy I don't want you confirming it.
'No problem,' he said with little will.

We returned with them at lunch time, sitting in the trailer hitched to the tractor. So much for health and safety. Jem standing up, despite my protests, to vanquish enemy's assailing us from every side. Stick in hand, pulled from the stone, he slayed the dragon, destroyed the infidel, routed the French and single handed, humbled the Hun all before lunch. His imagination was on fire and based on that line of logic I put the visitor and his watch down to an over active imagination for now. Careering into the yard, we hit a wall of baking smells that stopped us in our tracks. 'Play it cool lads,' announced Eamon, 'I'll go on an oul charm offence and secure us a bun or two or even three.'

'Each,' said Jem.
'Maybe pushing our luck there,' admitted Eamon. We entered like caster sugar wouldn't dissolve in our mouths. Eileen sat guard at the shop door. Piled up behind her on the counter an array of pies, cakes and buns stared back at us. Defeat grabbed us by the throat.

That night Johnnie, Sean and three locals, I only remember them as that, sat playing cards at the kitchen table. My Ma and May talking at the range. We the "children" were in the good room occupying ourselves as best we could.

'Uncle Johnnies taking us fishing after Mass,' crowed Jem. 'I'm going to catch a twenty pounder.'
'He's not you're real uncle,' I reminded him. 'He said I could call him uncle.'

'It's not the same ok,' I snarled back. I was at my wits end. Most of the afternoon and early evening I had been on Jem duty. Dragging him down from walls, stopping him from climbing drain pipes and apple trees. Warning about the danger of the lough. He didn't take a blind bit of notice. I was exhausted. Every so often Eileen would whisper something in his ear. He'd smirk over at me, the devil child looking out at me from behind his eyes.

We all rose early on Sunday for Mass. Nine of us, spit and polished, piled into the Ford. Four crammed onto the front bench seat, four on the back with Jem on the floor. If you have to stand on him, you can, called my Ma from the front. I'm not arriving at Latton Chapel with him hanging out the window like something from St Pats. St Pats being the Belfast equivalent of the English Borstal. She had tried earlier to get me to serve Mass with Father Ignatius but Johnnie came to my rescue, saying the Chapel already had fourteen perspective priests and brothers vying for spots on Sunday's.

'The competitions fierce,' said May. 'Some of them is dropping the children off at six in the morning so they can claim to be more pious than the others. Sure wasn't Seanie McCardle caught pitching a two man tent in McElroy's field at the back of the Chapel. So Sean Og would be up and at the door before the others.'

The roads around the Chapel were crammed. Gone are those days. Chaperoned by my Ma and May at the front and Johnnie at the back we filed in to a pew two back from the altar rails. Latton isn't a grand Chapel. It's got a bit of the Protestant about it. Simple, it's like that Ronseal slogan "it does what says on the tin". You could feel in touch with God, while still being comfortable. The big places, Cathedrals and the like, while stirring a sense of wonder left me isolated almost feeling insignificant. If they were Gods house and he had a lot of them, then clearly there was a distance between him and the peasants like me. I had some sympathy for the reformers position, though I thought smashing windows and chopping heads of statues was being overzealous. All that, you shall not make craven images, was all a bit to fundamentalist.

Father Ignatius, with seven on the altar tripping over themselves, nearly killed us. An hour and seventeen minutes. A record Sean said later.

Though, how he knew I don't know, as I caught him stealing out through the side door after the Word of the Lord. Fifteen minutes of the service was taken up drawing attention to us fine children from Belfast. A speech wherein he called us poor children, tortured and traumatised by the murderous troubles in the North. Which he followed with three decades of the Rosary for our safe keeping. After which, my Ma signed the three of us outside with a nod of her head, before the rest of the congregation left.

She lined us up along the chapel wall like victims of a firing squad, so we could shake hands and answer questions fired at us like bullets. Your name, your age, place of birth, the school you attended, and the games of sport you played, at the end of which we would all have happily signed our own death warrants. I was told later by Eamon, it was all done to assure the gathered Aunt Mary was bringing us up right, despite being beaten and battered by them Unionist bigots in the Six Counties.

We spent another half an hour hanging round the gates, while our adults gossiped with other adults. My Ma was a great hit and had invitations to tea to beat the band.

'We'll not get round them all May,' she lamented. 'We can if you'll stay on another few days,' says she with little or no concern for my sanity. Eileen gave her daggers. The country life was not for her it appeared. As for Jem, who had to be dragged away from one of the Celtic crosses, adorning a former parish priests grave, another few days, weeks, months probably meant nothing.

'Are we going fishing Uncle Johnnie,' Jem asked but the joie de vivre had gone out of his tone.
'We are, just as soon as we get back. The fish will still be there, they're not going anywhere.' Turning left at the cross we passed Clegg Lake. 'That's a bottomless lake,' said Johnnie. 'If you were to dive in there and keep swimming you'd come out in Australia. Two Australian fellows were found swimming in it last summer,' he added, a grin on him like Batman's Joker. 'The Garda arrested them as illegal aliens.' 'What like aliens from outer space?' asked Eileen. 'Sort of,' said Johnnie. May tutted.

Having arrived back the pot was put on, while we got out of our Sunday best. Eamon and Seamus gathered up a few rods and lines to be shared between us. The bait to be a pair of small perch Eamon had caught on a couple of static lines, he had cast out the night before.
'We'll put these boys on with a float and drift them behind the boat,' he said. 'The pike won't be able to resist them.'
'I bet I catch the first one,' announced Seamus in a tone designed to rebuke any other similar assertion and to irritate Eamon. 'In your dreams,' he countered. We walked down to the shoreline and with all of us pulling together, we turned the boat on to her keel,

pushing her through the shoreline gravel stern first, into the shallow water. She floated up and we tied her to a large branch hanging into the lough. It had come down in a previous storm.

Eamon set the rods on the ground while we waited for Johnnie.

It had turned out to be a beautiful day. The lough lightly rippled, sparkled, the smallest hint of a breeze slid by, caressing our skin with fingers of mink. The sky Cote d'azur, dotted sparingly with small fluffy clouds.

'It's warm for fishing,' offered Eamon. 'The heat drives the fish down to the cooler water. We'll be hard pushed to catch anything today.'

Just then Johnnie appeared.

'I'll get aboard first to steady her, and I'll do the rowing,' says he.

'Eamon and Jem you're at the bow and you two at the stern. Rule one, no moving about on the boat. Rule two, I'm in charge and whatever I say goes,' he added with the authority of a man who knows his place.

We did as he bid, pushing her out a few yards with Johnnie in the middle to get some deep water under her. Eamon and Jem clambered aboard taking up their seats at the front. Eamon carried the rods. We climbed on board and sat down quickly. Not a life vest in sight. With the tip of an oar Johnnie pushed us gently into deeper water before locking the oars into the rowing gates. Swiftly and in complete control he turned her about face and began with an easy expert stroke pushing us up the lough to the Cavan end. Eamon passed us a rod with the hook expertly baited. 'I've had to set the float at about twenty feet, so watch the line doesn't get tangled. That will hopefully get us into cool water,' explained Eamon.

Seamus shook his head. We moved with consummate ease over the water, it giving little resistance to Johnnies powerful stokes. The only sounds were the slush of the oars as they sliced the water's surface and the creak of the oarlocks twisting back and forth in their mountings.

We sat with our own thoughts. For my part, not to sound all Buddha like, I found I was at peace with myself and the world. Maybe, in such idyllic moments we all have the same thoughts. I wondered, if at some moment in time it was possible for the whole of humanity to have the same thought. If so, I wished it to be that moment.

I put my hand in the water. Given the talk of it being too warm for fishing it was colder than I expected. Somewhere among the reeds a Water Hen cried, warning of strangers approaching. In a field cresting a distant hill, tipped by small trees, several cows like miniatures chewed the cud. Walking factories, taking in raw materials to be processed, adding line value and then delivered as precious goods. Occasionally, above our heads Barn Swallow whistled by, twisting and turning as they fed on the wing. A parade of ducks skirted along the reeds on the far bank paddling furiously to make their escape. A Heron standing on the Point with heavy strained stokes raised itself, turning away from us crying foul at our disruption.

Thirty yards from the bank, Johnnie dipping one oar while raising the other out of the water, turned us not quite on a sixpence but more a two bob bit. He had turned us into the wind.

'It's a light breeze but we will drift nicely nonetheless,' he explained, 'there's a natural current on the lough running east. We think she has a secret outlet down at the Rock that maintains her at the same level no matter the weather. If we move to fast I'll pull the boat back a little.'

Her and she. Maybe I had picked it up from him in the past.

We cast our lines left and right. The floats bobbed cheerfully on the ripples. Ours green and white, the other blue and white. Celtic versus Rangers I thought. With whispered voices we talked of past successes. The time I caught a two pound bream with a bamboo and string jerry rigged by Uncle Jim. The Sunday in May, when Sean caught a forty pound pike at the Point and found a baby duck in its belly.

'There's none of those monsters left,' complained Eamon. 'The Germans have them, either in their bellies or stuffed on their walls.' Johnnie again told us the story of John Devlin and the Devil. I'd heard it on each visit but it was always worth the listening, given he embellished it each time. Like the fish always gets bigger, as the fisherman retells the story about the one that got away.

We had drifted half way with what looked like the occasional nibble. Jem had become surprisingly quiet.

'What's up with him,' whispered Seamus. I didn't know. Even going to Mass that morning he seemed quiet. Even distracted.

'I think it's because he hasn't caught anything,' I suggested but I wasn't convinced.

Over the next two hours, Johnnie letting us drift fifty yards or so, would then draw us back twenty or thirty yards each time, until at last we reached the near shore and the roof line of the house came into view.

'That's it lads,' he announced. 'There's work to be done. Rosemary is away with Sean to Clones so you lads will have to get the cows.'

Jem didn't even squeak. Turning the bow with four further strokes he run the boat up on to the shore. The gravel grating under us. We handed our rod to Eamon who wound both in, all of us hoping in those last submerged moments there would be a taker. Disappointment reined. We trudged back to the house.

'Change your boots and come in for some tea or a mineral,' called Johnnie as we four made our way to the storehouse door. Johnnies two having changed quickly and left, I sat on the mattress as Jem stood with his back to me looking out the window.

'He was back,' he said. 'Who?'
'The wet fella, he was here this morning again.' 'Did he speak to you?'
'No he was pacing around the room. Real agitated. Talking to himself, it was all funny talk. All I could make out was the watch and the cupboard.'
'Did you speak to him?' 'No.'
'Are you sure you weren't dreaming.'
He turned, his eyes wild and staring.
'Yes I'm sure. Did you not see him at the lake?' It was my turn to say no.
'He was standing on that place that sticks out.' 'The Point. I didn't see him. I saw a bird, a Heron.'
'I tell you it was him he was on the water's edge waving at us, at me, calling out.'
'What was he saying?'

'I don't know, I couldn't hear the words over the wind, the rain was beating on me, blinding me.' Without warning he slumped down on the floor with a thump. Jumping up I took hold of him and laid him on the mattress. Throwing the blankets over him even though he was burning, I bounded down the stair calling for my Ma. A gang appeared at the door. 'It's Jem he's sick, he's really sick, he's burning.'

My Ma and May barging by me, reminiscent of St. John's Ambulance on manoeuvres, pounded up the stair like young ones.

'Stay here,' demanded Johnnie taking control of the rest of us. 'You, off and get the cows,' he snapped at the two boys, they turned and moved away.

'Eileen dear will you go in and put the pot on the range. Jem will need some hot drinks to help get his fever down.' Reluctant at first he moved her on with the tilt of his head and a smile.

He turned on me.

'What's going on? I stuttered meaningless words.

'Has he been talking to someone?'

I froze. Yes or no he demanded. 'Yes.'

'How many times?' 'Three I think.'

'God damn it,' he groaned putting his hand to his face pulling at the skin. 'When was the first time. What happened?'

'He said he woke to find him sitting on the bed.'

'When?

'Yesterday.'

'Was he wet,' he fired at me.

'I thought he had wet the bed that's why I didn't say anything.'

'No, no not Jem the visitor, the apparition was he wet.'

'Yes. I saw his footprints.' 'You're sure.'

'Yes. Jem said he was soaking. He was talking about a watch in a cupboard or something. I just thought Jem was at his tricks.'

'That's understandable,' he offered, as some comfort, realising I was adrift with fear and concern.

'And the other times.'
'This morning before Mass and on the Point this afternoon. Where the Heron rose.'
'It's true then,' he whispered. 'What's, what's true.'
'I'll explain later. The main thing is not to let Jem out of our sight for the next few days.'
'Would we be better taking him home?' 'No, it's started we have to finish it here.' 'What's started?'

'Look, I will tell you later. I'm going for Father Ignatius. You stay upstairs with Jem. No matter what happens you stay with him. Do you hear me?' 'No matter what happens stay with him,' he roared over his shoulder as he ran for the Ford, his words beating me about the face and head. Momentarily frozen, I shook myself and raced up the steps slamming the door at the head of the stair. 'Johnnie says I'm to stay with him.'
'He'll be all right,' said May rising from the mattress. 'Come with me we'll get him some broth.'
'No, I'm to stay here. Johnnie said I am not to leave. No matter what happens,' I reaffirmed. The effect on May was palpable. Covering her mouth with her hand she touched me on my shoulder.

'He's gone for the priest,' I added.

My Ma startled by the revelation rose. 'Priest, priest sure it's just a fever.'

'Come with me Mary,' demanded May her voice that of the uncompromising.

'What's happening May.' 'Let's go into the house Mary.'

My Ma bewildered looked down on Jem.

'The men have it under control. Let's go now Mary.'

My Ma followed wordless. I made sure the door was closed firmly and locked before sitting down on the windowsill.

Jem was restless. Making sharp short turns in the bed. The occasional whine or grunt coming from him.

It was one and a half hours before Johnnie returned. Father Ignatius was on house calls. He had waited for him but in the end had to leave word an urgent call was required. By the time of his return the cows had been and gone. The night was closing in earlier than expected, the sky had blackened. Eamon and Seamus sat with me. Eileen had been banded from the room, having personally accused me of trying kill Jem by allowing him on the boat without a jumper. I put it down to hormones.

Johnnie entering the room looked worn. He dragged an old trunk out and sat down on it. 'What's up Da,' asked Seamus more serious than I had ever seen him. 'You recall me telling you about the drowning here, when Sean was just younster.'

'Oul Padraig,' said Seamus.

'Yes, well it seems the Devils words are coming true. Many a time I've told you John Devlin's story of meeting the Devil at the Hut Cross. But I've never told you what John said were the Devils parting words.'

Outside a door slammed we jumped like Olympic hurdlers.

'The Devil told him good fortune wasn't free. A price was payable to him and he would in good time collect what was owed to him. He said the Heron would cry three times. It's been twenty years, I think he's coming to collect.'

'You mean Jem,' I asked. 'Why him, he's not from here. Is the fever going to kill him?'

'Not a fever. Tell us again, everything he said to you, every detail no matter how small or seemingly insignificant.'

So I told him. Eamon and Seamus mouths open sat transfixed.

'We need to find the cupboard, that's where the watch has to be,' said Eamon. 'That's if it even exists.'

'Maybe oul Padraig is warning us through reference to watch, that time is running out,' suggested Seamus.

'There could be something in that. But is he trying to forewarn us or is he simply passing on a message for another,' speculated Johnnie.

The door rapped, we lost our lives momentarily. It was Father Ignatius.

'I got here as soon as I could John,' he apologised. 'Old O'Reilly is on his last legs. All he has is Jane and her in a worse state than him. I had to stay with them. What's the urgency, what's happened?

Twenty five minutes later Johnnie finished his explanation, during which time the priest blessed himself seven times and called on Mary the Holy Mother of Jesus half a dozen times to save us.

'Have you any idea where this cupboard might be,' he asked.

'I can only think it's at Patsy's old house. The place has been empty this five year since he passed away.'

'Then we have to go there,' announced Ignatius. 'When.'

'Tonight we can't waste a minute. You and I will go. The boys can stay with Jem. Lock the door lads and keep the lights lit. Let no one in, no matter who they claim to be. No one you hear me. Watch out for us coming back. John you need to tell May to lock up the house and keep all the lights on.'

He pulled his black trench coat on and taking from the pocket a crumpled hat he pulled it down tight over his ears. He looked half crazy. From the other pocket he produced a small bottle. Unscrewing the lid he took a drink and then sprinkled some around Jem's mattress.

'Holy water,' asked Eamon.

'Whiskey and a blessing,' said the priest. 'Thank God for inventing whiskey is all I can say. John wrap up well there's a storm coming I can feel it in my bones. It seems the boyo himself has a bone to pick with us.'

Opening the door he strode down the stair, Johnnie followed struggling into a heavy coat. We slammed and locked the door. A few minutes later we heard the Ford ripping out of the yard and down the road.

The hours past. I lay awake on the mattress. Outside the wind and rain beat rhythms on the window. Angry violent tunes.
'Jesus Christ preserve us,' said Eamon. 'Father Ignatius was right. It hasn't blew like this in living memory. The roofs will be off in morning.' 'It's the banshee,' cried Seamus from under the blankets.
'Hold your whist,' snapped Eamon, 'you'll wake the young one with your squawking.'

Jem lay sleeping. Unconscious of the terror around him.
'The banshee,' I asked. 'Like the banshee in Darby O'Gill.'
'Don't listen to him,' said Eamon digging Seamus. Seamus popping his head out wailed, 'she was here before, sent to collect our Grandad. Ask your Ma she knows. The storms just a cover, she'll be here soon.' Rising I double checked the door.

'That won't stop her. It's not her you need to fear, she's just the messenger. It's the one that comes after her.'

I looked out the window, the fingers of light from the yard lights lit the trees lining the water's edge. They swayed in the wind, like some sort of voodoo dancers. The wind wailing in their boughs, tore small branches off and shredded leaves. I didn't hear the Ford but saw her lights as she rounded the bend at the Rock.

Johnnie threw her into the yard.
We heard someone clatter up the stair. 'Who is it,' called Eamon.
'It's your Da open up.'
Despite being told to let no one in, he let them in. 'Who are you,' I asked just to be safe, 'are you the Devils disciples.'

'In some ways Martin we are all the Devil's disciples,' retorted Father Ignatius, 'but not tonight.' They looked dishevelled. Their hair tossed and tangled, the overcoats as they pulled them off seemed twisted and gnarled. Thinking now of them, they were like those plasticine figures kids make that have been pulled out of shape but are just recognisable despite their distortion.
'Did you find the cupboard,' queried Eamon.
'We did,' replied Johnnie. 'It was in the back room. A tall black thing. Patsy must have bought it or made it. I don't recall it being there in Padraig's time.' He opened his hand to reveal a pocket watch.
At first I thought it only had one hand but realised the two hands read eleven fifty five.

'It must have stopped at the very hour and minute poor Padraig disappeared,' offered Johnnie. 'I remember the night, hearing Patsy Jim Pats voice roaring over the wind. I looked at the clock on the mantel. It was a quarter to twelve. By the time I got the coat and boots on and ran to the lake it was ease five minutes. When I arrived he was up to his knees pleading with Padraig who was just sitting in the boat. I waded out and as I did so Patsy struggled out up to his waist. It was all I could do to haul him back, him being a small but wiry wee man. We fell backwards onto the bank just as the mist enveloped the boat. That was it. The storm abated. Patsy lay sobbing on the grass. Taking him inside I roused May. We got whiskey and heat into ourselves and dried off by the range. At around six, he and I with Jack McCabe in tow searched the lough. We found the boat beached up at the Point.'

'Where we saw and heard the Heron and Jem saw the apparition again,' I said.
'For the third time,' added Johnnie. 'What time is it now,' asked Eamon.
'It's just gone ten, so we have an hour and fifty five minutes,' replied the Priest.
'Are you sure it's tonight,' asked Eamon, 'what date was it when Padraig drown,'
'July 15th, 1952, confirmed Johnnie
'My Ma was born on July 15th 1932,' I interrupted.
We are coming to that said the priest. I was taken aback.

'Its the 20th of July today, isn't it,' asked Johnnie. 'I'm a bit confused with all the goings on,' he added. 'So it's more than twenty years till today.

You'd think the Devil would be a bit more prompt.' 'With so many wanton souls to collect nowadays,' said Father Ignatius, 'I can understand why he is running a bit late.' He said it with some maliciousness, not towards the Devil but at those of his flock who failed to listen to his message. We didn't look him in the eye.

'It's the leap years,' said Eamon pleased with himself. 'I can't imagine Beelzebub being tardy about accounting for souls. He doesn't seem the sort. If you'll forgive me Father, from what you have taught us he seems like a calculating sort of individual. We have had five leap years including this year. For some reason he added in the extra days.'

'Very generous of him,' spat Seamus.
'So it is tonight,' I confirmed. Though the penny had already dropped with all present.

'There's also this,' said Father Ignatius, pulling from the inside pocket of his jacket a bundle of papers. 'We found it in the cupboard. It was like a little shrine to Padraig. Patsy had obviously gathered things up as memento. In the cupboard was the pocket watch, his cap, a couple of medals, his missal and a few letters from his brother in America.'

'What's the document say,' I asked. 'You should sit down Martin.'

I dropped down on the empty mattress. Was it me he was really after? Had he mistaken Jem for me? 'You will recall being told many years ago, that Patsy's wife Mary died in child birth. After that he and oul Padraig were inseparable.

Even as Padraig's mind went. Well there was good reason. On the night Mary died, the doctor having given his prognosis mother and child were doomed and my predecessor Father Malachy having given the last rites, Padraig disappeared.'

'Father Malachy, it was his grave we had to drag Jem off after mass this morning,' uttered Seamus. 'The same. When Padraig returned Mary was dead but the baby girl was alive. A miracle they all thought. The baby was given over to a family to bring up as theirs, as there was no way Patsy could rear her on his own.'

'It was not uncommon in them days,' proffered Johnnie looking at me through the corner of his eye. I hung on their every word, a weight of realisation beginning to sit on me. I moved to speak but the priest raised his hand.

'As the years went by Padraig's mind began to go. It was all Patsy could do to get sense out of him. But bit by bit he pieced the story together. He scribbled it down on these pages. Padraig had gone to the Hut Cross to invoke the Devils intercession, God he felt had abandoned his favourite nephew and his wife. He had already signed over all his worldly possessions to them, why not give them his life. That night, in return for one soul he sold his. The Devil drove a hard bargain, one for one and twenty years. Padraig pleaded with him to spare the two and he would go in ten but to no avail. He had to choose mother or child. He even offered himself there and then but the Devil wanted his pleasure. So Padraig chose the baby and the mother died in that instance. Despite saving the child, it would appear he was riddled with guilt. Had he tried hard enough, had he made the right choice? The guilt maybe drove him insane. Several times he tried to kill himself. But it was like he had a guardian angel looking out for him. We now know it was the Devil. Maximising his pleasure. Causing grieve for uncle and nephew.'

'The baby, what was the baby called,' I asked already knowing. Ignatius looked at Johnnie.

'Mary. The baby was called Mary, my sister, your mother,' admitted Johnnie.
I was floored. Inside my head no rational thought. Numb, lost, angry are words I think of now but even they are figments of this age not then. I was brought back by Johnnie shaking me by the shoulder.
'Whatever you're thinking, whatever questions you have forget them for now. We have one task, all of us, to save Jem,' he ordered.
'I can't tell you why the Devil chose him but choose him he has,' said Father Ignatius. 'In an hour and

twenty minutes he is coming here to collect and we are going to stop him.'

'Eamon and Seamus surely they can go,' I pleaded. 'They can join my Ma and the others in the house. He has no interest in them.'

'I'll stay,' piped Eamon, 'it's not every day you get to meet the Devil.'

Less brazen Seamus nodded his agreement.

'Was there nothing in the cupboard or even that document that gives a clue why he's looking another life, a deals a deal,' I asked.

'It's the Devil we are talking about here,' noted Ignatius.

'There is something Father,' said Johnnie who now stood facing the door his back to us.

'What, what spit it out,' snapped Ignatius? Turning he was as white as a bed sheet.

'Mary wasn't the only child born that night,' she had a twin brother. The Devil, he feels cheated I guess.'

'Who took the child, was it a local family,' I asked.

'No, Father Malachy and Doctor Norton took him. The Doctor knew a wet nurse. He left the boy with her. Later, Father Malachy arranged for a family to take the twin. He told no one where the baby was. Years later, on his deathbed, he told Patsy the child had gone to a good home in his native town.'

'Belfast,' I said. 'Yes.'

'The child, its Jem's father Malachy. Named after the priest who saved him,' I almost roared.

'Talk about the sins of the father,' huffed Eamon. 'So Padraig stroked him. Got one over on the Devil. You don't see that every day,' cracked Seamus.

'You do in my profession,' retorted Father Ignatius. It raised a smile among us.

'The madness, maybe it wasn't brought on by guilt after all but by fear the boy would be found,' suggested Seamus.

'The apparitions, they're to warn us he is coming. The wet fella, as Jem calls him, isn't his messenger it isn't even Padraig, its Patsy. Patsy protecting his grandson,' said Johnnie.

'We have an hour. I want you all out,' demanded the Priest, who seemed emboldened by all he now knew. I knew it was coming.

'All out except you Martin,' he added. 'Not a chance,' hissed Johnnie.

'John I haven't time to explain. Just do what I say. Will you stay Martin?'

I nodded.

'Get Jem into the house, put these in his hands,' he said producing a set of Rosary Beads from his trouser pocket. 'They're from Rome, blessed by His Holiness Pope Paul the Sixth himself.' Kissing them he handed them over.

Jem swaddled in a blanket was lifted feather light and taken out. Johnnie looking over his shoulder at me as he went, followed by Seamus.

'I'll stay Father,' offered Eamon.

'Thank you it's a brave offer but I need to limit his targets and you being here could give him ammunition against me. I can't afford that. The elements are stacked against us already.' He patted Eamon on the back.

'Tell that Father of yours and Mary no matter what they hear or see not to leave the house. Tell them to have the pot on. And a wee dram,' he called after Eamon as he descended. Closing the door he bolted it. 'That's more to keep us in Martin than to keep him out.'

For a moment my senses got the better of me. I had visions of Father Ignatius transforming into Old Nick.

Looking at his watch he announced we had forty minutes. He suggested we make ourselves comfortable. A tall order. Pulling the little bottle from his jacket pocket he gave it a shake.

'Only a mouthful left. I fear I've been a bit heavy handed with the shaking. Maybe I should have drunk more of it. For Dutch courage, I mean. Do you know why they call it Dutch courage,' he asked.

'I assume you have some sort of plan Father,' I asked. I didn't need Dutch courage just an assurance that the alleged adult among us had a plan of action.

'I can't lie to you Martin. I haven't a plan as such, it's more a hunch. When I say a hunch I mean a sort of educated guess.'

'Do you intend to let me in on it Father?' 'No.'

'No,' I replied with incredulity.

'No. If I am right and I think I am the less you know the better.'

'That doesn't fill me with confidence.'

'Listen I believe, though some theologians have argued the counter, that the Devil doesn't know us personally. God knows us intimately as our maker and his. In his falling from grace he took sin as his weapon but not knowledge. For the Devil to enter us we need to invite him in To sin. Even then his knowledge of us is only our sins. Padraig wasn't any more a sinner than the rest of us. But he invited the Devil in to make a bargain.'

'For a good cause,' I suggested.

That's for another day's discussion.' He looked at his watch. 'Twenty two minutes.'

'Without his sin I would not be here,' I protested.

'Without sin a lot of us would not be here, mark my words. I was going to pray Martin,' he continued, 'but the gravity of our situation, seems for once, to make praying too small.'

I didn't responded. The Devil was calling and the local priest was losing his faith. From the right hand pocket of his jacket he took a Stole and a small bottle. Placing the former around his neck, he opened the bottle pouring some of the contents on to his right hand. He blessed himself and then me. I noticed the tremble in his hands.

'More whiskey Father.'

'Olive oil it's used to anoint the sick and the dying,' he replied, instantly regretting it.

Outside the storm was abating. The clock ticked down. We sat with our own thoughts. I had so many, all in a jumble I don't recall them clearly.

The footsteps on the stair brought us both back. We could hear the wood creaking on the little landing in front of the door. A light rap, followed by another slightly more pronounced. We didn't move or speak. Then he stepped in. Straight through the bolted door.

'Did you not hear me knocking,' he asked. 'I hope I am not disturbing you. Just I have come to collect something that belongs to me. If the boy will just come with me now Father, I'll be on my way. No need for anyone to make a scene.'

We sat open mouthed, prettified like fossils.
His demeanour was courteous almost subservient. He was quite handsome. The ladies would have liked him. The tanned skin, the full head of hair. Tidy little ears, strong lips. His black suit neat, clearly tailored. It was the white shirt that threw me. It looked Ben Sherman with a button down collar but clearly wasn't, as it had cuff links. Two little silver dice. I imagined it would be red like the one the devil wore in Bedazzled.

He smiled.
'You can close your mouths,' he said. 'I suppose you were expecting Bulgakov's devil. I am sorry to disappoint you.'

'Will you not sit down and talk a while with us,' said Ignatius a clear tremble in his opening words.

'I suppose I can spare you a few minutes Father, as I won't be seeing you again for quite a few years.'

He sat on the trunk, dusting it off with his hand before sitting. Clearly no tail. He caught me looking and smiled at me. An inviting, fatherly smile.

'I was hoping this might be our only encounter,' replied Ignatius.

'I'm afraid not Ignatius. But let's not talk of the future. Clearly you feel there are some grounds why the fine young man should not be given into my charge. I feel most upset by all of this. Hence the storm and all that palaver. I was a bit miffed, sorry about that.'

'That's ok Lucifer,' said Father Ignatius like he was forgiving the taking of an apple. 'May I call you Lucifer?'

'Feel free Father I am called worse,' he smiled at us, his teeth pearly white.

'I was cheated Father. I acted in good faith with Padraig. He got Mary, who I see is in the house. An attractive woman. A deals a deal,' he huffed. 'It is I agree. He got the girl and twenty years and you got the mother. That was the deal was it not.' 'But the boy, Father,' he smiled over at me. The young man's parent shouldn't have been here and so the boy shouldn't be either. He's an anomaly. It puts everything out of kilter. Here I am, in some god forsaken corner of this little impoverished island, no offence intended Father, tracking down a non-life. I should be out sinking boats, crashing planes, assassinating presidents but here I am talking to a lowly parish priest and a non-life. No offence again Father.'

'None taken Lucifer.'

Silence sat with us. The Devil looked around the room. Clearly the surroundings were not to his taste. 'Can I ask you something Lucifer,' said Father Ignatius.

'Be my guest,' he replied.

'Do you ever have doubts, do you ever wake up and think it's wrong, what I am doing is wrong. I need to mend my ways. Ask God for forgiveness. Ask to be given another chance.'

He looked back at us his face not incredulous, just bemused I suppose.

'Doubts, I'm not sure what you mean Father. God's forgiveness. Why would I ask him for forgiveness? It was him who appointed me in the first place. I think there must be some misunderstanding. I didn't ask for this job, he created it.'

'So all that stuff about you falling from grace and heavenly wars and serpents.'

'A cover story,' he replied pursing his lips and shaking his head in a sort of brother Gerry gay way. 'All made up I'm afraid.'

'I don't understand,' whispered Father Ignatius clearly disturbed by what he was hearing.

'He was bored.'

We looked back confused.

'God. The whole humanity thing, the garden of Eden, peace, love, harmony. He said he was bored with it all. He wanted to spice it up a bit. Though, I don't think he realised at the time what he was unleashing. It was all new to him. To all of us. We were just sitting one day and he says, Lucifer would you be interested in a new job. I was head of the Angels at the time. It will have to be our secret he says. I need you to go rogue. I hadn't a clue what he was on about. Then he just laid it out for me. Murder, pestilence, plaques, wars, gambling, pornography, how could I refuse. It all sounded so exhilarating. Told me I would have my own place. I could call it what I liked. Hell. That was me, I came up with that.'
'It's certainly catchy alright,' said Ignatius.

'So you see Father, just like you I am doing his work. He's pleased with it all so far, though one or two events have shaken him a bit. Those world wars, the starvation and famines. He has asked me to tone those down a bit.'
'The Holocaust,' asked Ignatius. The Devil didn't reply.

'The Spanish Inquisition,' now he thought that was pure genius,' he said shaking with delight.
'So all this Christianity stuff, being good, helping ones neighbour, it's all nonsense then.'
'No, no Father. There's a balance to be kept. To be fair to him, he did emphasis from the start we had to strike a balance between good and fun.'

'Fun!'

'Yes fun that's what we call it. Look I know down here you call it evil, the Devils work but to us it's just.... fun.'

'The suffering, the pain, the dying, fun.'

'Father, look at it from our perspective, we gave you the earth, free will, food, intelligence, alcohol. We raised you up above the other animals. Listen, prior to my appointment you were twenty different types of monkeys, Homo Abilis, Homo erectus, Homo Neanderthal and so on. In fact, God thought the Neanderthals were his finest creation. I suggested we look at some of the others. Neanderthals and fun it just didn't work for me. I suggested Homo sapiens, though you were still a bit, dare I said it, a bit thick at the time. Said he would leave it to me. Thinking about it, fire, I think fire was the coolest think I gave you. It really set you guys apart. Kings of the jungle and all that.'

'You invented fire.'

'Bet your bottom dollar I did. Sorry, I just love that line. What was that… that film. Oh I hate it when you can't remember something.

God says I have too much on my mind. I need to relax more. Take a break. It's just not that easy these days. With regional wars and famine in Africa. Then there's the Cold War. Don't really want it going to cold, so one day I'm in Russia.

Twenty four hours later, I'm talking in the ear of some red neck Republican Senator in Washington, who wants to nuke the ruskies.

Sometimes, I just think, go ahead press the button what do I care. But God he reminds me, Luci we need to maintain the balance between good and fun. So he sends down these so called good people like Mother Teresa, Ghandi, Joan of Arc and that little fellow, nice chap, the Dalai Lama.' 'And you counter balance them with?' queried the Father.

'I suppose you're going to say Hitler and Stalin and so on,' growled the Devil though in a sort of pussy cat way.

'They did cross my mind and others,' retorted Ignatius.

'Remember free will. I just said to them look have a bit of fun. I didn't tell them to start world wars, to deport millions to Siberia and the gulags.'

'And the gas chambers,' He didn't answer.

'My job is to present the opportunity for fun. How others interpret that is up to them.'

To this point I had sat in silence.

'Why sir. Why with all you have to do. All the fun you are having, why come after me. Surely I am insignificant in the overall scheme.'

He turned to face me. His eyes changing colour. 'A deals a deal Martin. Did you think you could fool me? I know Jem's in the house. By the way Father, the Rosary Beads won't save him. Pope Paul,' he scoffed. 'Popes are puppets of an earth bound church. At least the Protestants are right about one thing but that's about all. Religion was invented to control the masses. God didn't create religion you did. Jews, Hindus, Christian, Buddhists the list goes on. I didn't set you at each other's throats you did that yourselves.'

'We could discuss that at length if you wish,' suggested Father Ignatius, buying for time no doubt.

'I'm sure we could Father, your lot like nothing more than a long theological debate about Cessationism, the Hermeneutic Loop and other minutiae, while the world and everyone in it goes to hell in my hand cart.

'What is hell,' I suddenly asked.

'A good question young Martin given Jem's predicament. Its less than a day ago you would have sent him there yourself.'

'Thinking and doing are different things,' I replied.

'We have a young philosopher in our midst.'

'The young see the world in a different light to us. They see hope, the ability to change, immortality,' offered Father Ignatius in weak attempt I guess to draw the conversation out. 'Ah immortality. That's above my pay grade I'm afraid. You need to speak to him above,' he indicated upwards with his eyes to emphasis the point.

'Can we,' I asked. 'What.'

'Speak to him,' replied Father Ignatius.

'I thought you did so every day. Is that not what all that holier than thou stuff is about. Those boring masses, the Decades of the Rosary. If you only knew what he had to say about them. And that bible of yours.'

'His,' retorted Ignatius. Yours, written by men, censored by men, designed to manipulate and control the world of men through religion, a man made construct. Let me tell you this, God wouldn't recognise one of man's homespun parables from another.'

'It includes women,' offered the priest almost as some lame excuse to prove the value of the good books existence.

'I doubt they had little to do with it,' snapped the Devil. 'If they had let women have a say, maybe things might have turned out better for humanity.' 'I doubt it,' rebuked Father Ignatius. 'I have been a priest for forty years and nothing I have heard or seen of them tells me it would be any better.

We are all human. They have all the same human frailties. The ones you exploit.'

'Exploit. Oh that's cruel. What do you think I gain by your folly? Do you think I accumulate wealth, payment for every soul? Maybe points, like those, what are they called Green Shield Stamps. Collect five hundred get another set of wings. I get nothing. Except the satisfaction of doing my job well. A job my creator gave me.'

'Don't tell me you don't get a little thrill from the power,' goaded the Father. 'A little power crazy. Maybe once in a while nudge someone in the wrong direction.'

'What if I do, do you think he cares? If he was so concerned for you, for your souls,' he laughed.

'Souls I love it. I'm not sure who came up with that one. If he was concerned, if he cared one iota for his creations do you think he would have appointed me? You are no more than playthings, one of a hundred million things he has created. Universes within universes. A hundred billion stars and you think you are alone. His only concern. The naivety, the arrogance!'

'He sent his only begotten son for our salvation.' 'He sent him to get him out from under his feet. To teach him a little manners. You know he wasn't meant to be crucified.'
Father Ignatius smirked his disbelief.
'You look surprised. He told him he would send angels to lift him up in front of the masses. Forgot all about him. It was three days later when he remembered. You never heard anything like the moaning and whining that went on. Whipped this and thorns that, crucified and for what and to add insult to injury crucified with thieves and murderers. Both of whom by the way are with my lot now.'
'So he didn't die to save our sins,' I asked. 'He died because his father was on the lash with a crowd of his mates, at some Bacchanalian feast and slept in. What can I say, the place was full of them wood nymphs and fairies? Hard to resist all those naked breasts.' 'Not in front of the boy please,' requested Father Ignatius.
'Apologises. Look I have over stayed my welcome. I am going to nip downstairs, get the boy and go.'

'Hell,' I said, hell you were going to tell me what it is.'

'Well it isn't all that fire and brimstone nonsense. And in passing don't listen to this man and his lot spouting on about purgatory.

Doesn't exist,' he said shaking his head emphatically. Raising his finger he wagged it at the Father. 'Naughty, naughty. All made up Martin purgatorial indulgences were made up so the church hierarchy could live their lavish lifestyle.'

'Hells a state of mind. It's all the things you want but can't have. It's looking on while others have fun. Lust, envy, greed all the seven deadly sins and you can't fulfil any of them.'

'Take me,' I offered before realising the import of my utterance.

'Martin don't be hasty. I am sure we can talk this over, come to some arrangement,' proffered the Father.

'A deals a deal Father,' I replied firmly. He came for a boy, why not me. I am sure he doesn't care who it is, so long as he gets his man, boy.'

The Devil sat stirring at me his eyes shades of blue, grey and black sometimes red. He touched his lips with his tongue. I was disappointed it wasn't forked.

'I am just saying maybe it would be more fun to leave Jem here. Let him try and make his way through this crazy world. Based on what you have told us he seems better suited than me sir.'

'Tempting,' he whispered. 'You have placed me in a dilemma master Martin. I like your logic and the grand gesture. Jem, if I leave him I'm fairly certain I will get him in due course. But you, you're an unknown quantity, at least for now,' he smiled though there was nothing warm or pleasant about it. 'You have won some brownie points.'

'Jem or me then,' I announced.

'No, Jem, you or no one. Give me a moment to think.' He rose and walked to the window.

'You know I have been here once before. It was to collect your grandfather,' he said standing with his back to us. His words had a tone of fondest. My cancer got him. I am not entirely heartless. He was in pain. He wasn't a bad man, just unfortunate. It's a lottery.

'The banshee episode,' I said.

'Yes, it was a bit melodramatic I admit. Country people love all that folklore stuff. The place is so dull, I thought I would liven it up a bit. I think I scared the wits out of your mother. I knew who she was. Sort of tit for tat. Sorry,' he said turning to look at me. I think he even meant it.

'I'm not as bad as you all think. Certainly not as bad as your lot make out,' he scowled at Father Ignatius.

'So much of what goes on in this world is of your own doing,' he sighed.

'Apologises,' Ignatius replied.

'Martin I have decided. I know it's a hasty decision which I may regret....I will take you.'

My heart sank to my feet.

'Only kidding,' he spluttered. 'Fun, I told you it is all just fun. There will be a hole in the accounts but

I am sure I can fiddle the books a little, make the shortage up somewhere. I will go. Father I hope you will put a good word in for me with you colleagues.'

'You have given me food for thought,' offered the priest.

'Which reminds me, I haven't eaten seen eleven fifty five last night. I won't shake hands. I hate long good byes.'

He strode off through the door. The landing creaked and that was it.

I turned to look at the Priest, he was visibly shaking. A small patch of white hair had appeared on his head. The Devils singe, my Da said, when I recounted the story to him.

I helped him up.

'Good triumphed over evil today Martin.' The door of the store room blew open slamming against the wall. Looking at me Father Ignatius mouthed sorry.

'What about your hunch Father, were you right,' I asked him.

'No,' he admitted.

'And your lack of knowledge theory.'

'I think it needs more work,' he admitted.

'Damn it,' I said, 'I forgot to ask him about the leap years.

'Next time,' said the priest.

He looked at his watch, all three hands pointed to six. His little joke, I said bringing a smile to the Fathers face.

Making our way down the steps, we entered the yard to find it pristine, the detritus of the storm gone. Fair play to him, said the priest. Rapping on the front door of the farmhouse we identified ourselves. Dragged into the house, the door locked behind us, we found Jem sitting at the head of the table eating fried eggs and bacon.

'I was starving,' he said catching my look. 'Eat your fill,' I said.

Questions were flying.

'I think the Father needs that whiskey first Uncle Johnnie,' I suggested. 'And me can I have a ham and cheese sandwich and tea.'

My Ma hugged me. The Devil said sorry I whispered to her.

By eight I was exhausted by my ordeal and the questions. Johnnie drove Father Ignatius back to the parochial house. He said on parting he would pray for us all.

I awoke the next morning, having slept for twenty four hours, to the news Jem's father, actually his step father, had died in his sleep. Sometime around twelve midnight.

My Ma confided in me it was a relief. He was a brute of a man, forever lifting his hand to wife and children. Jem's birth father Malachy, her twin brother, had died when Jem was only three. She said, even though she knew she was adopted, she never felt it, but she did feel there was something missing in her life. Now she knew.

Given the trauma of the few days we decided to go home early. We couldn't face a funeral, not in our fragile state and asked Johnnie to pass on apologises. Though, they didn't show it, the Connolly's at the lough were glad to see us go and probably rightly so. Tommy was summoned and arrived late in the afternoon. Once again, the Swallows packed up, roof rack full, six Bantam eggs for my Da in the glove box, we headed home.

Crossing the border once more, Jem waking from a sleep on Eileen's shoulder asked if we were home yet.

Two years later I received a letter post marked Greece. It was from Father Ignatius now Brother Gabriel. He had left the priesthood citing personal reasons and joined the monastic life at Mount Athos. "In truth," he wrote "I am hiding from the sins of the world."

Jem went on to excel in school, went to university, read law and became a solicitor. While a little flamboyant and vocal for the times, he was highly regarded by his peers. He built a good criminal law reputation, married a practical girl, and started a family, settling down to the routine of middle class life. He was murdered in front of his family by the UVF on July 25th 1992. Twenty years (and the Leap days). It transpired later his killers had been fed information about his movements by the forces of the great English democratic State. One of potentially dozens of state sanctioned murders.

We didn't need the Devil to sin.

The Gripes of Ralph

There were two things my Da couldn't stand about his half-sisters husband, the first was his name, Ralph and the second was his constant complaining. Oh, he also couldn't stand him because he was English. So three things. But the latter was taken as read and didn't need to be repeated, at least not that often. Not often being once a month. What would you expect, sure he is English, was generally tagged at every mention of Ralph's latest gripe. My Grandad said Ralph was the worst type of English man in that he was still alive. He would chuckle with mire at that joke, which had run its course probably two years earlier.

His full name was Ralph James Casey. I should mention, even worse than all of the above, he was a born again Christian. His father James had been an ordained minister in some obscure English missionary sect but had fallen like the Angel Samael. He spent his early ministerial years in the US, proselytising the youth of the mid-west. It was the nineteen thirties. He had returned penniless and dissolutioned by life and God, the noose of his collar slackened and on return discarded. Ralph claimed, it was the suffering and degradation he had witnessed of the whites, across America's dust bowl, that broke him. Degradation, that had lowered the whites to a non-human state almost equivalent to the Negro's natural state, he added. By the way he was also a racist. He had clearly never seen an Edwardian London slum.

He recalled the plight of one family his father encountered. The Jones or Joads. I am no longer certain of the name. Who having lost their tenanted farm to the droughts, dust storms and banks, like a mini tribe made their way west to the land of milk and honey, California. Like the Indian tribes of a century earlier driven from their lands by the ancestors of the Jones or Joads. The old ones dying on the way. Buried in deep holes so animals and perhaps humans couldn't smell them and dig them up for sustenance. Traipsing through desert and dissension like modern day Mexican immigrants. The Mexicans, tracing in reverse the steps of their forefathers.

Ralph had an opinion on everything, as of course did my Da. Ralph's was one based on the misguided believe, that everything British or more precisely, everything English and Christian was superior. It seemed Ralph, as a reaction to the life of debauchery his father led on returning to England, took up religion with the zeal of a fundamentalist. His having married my Aunty Evelyn was a sacrifice. She was a devout women, her knees hardened and calloused from spending so much time on them praying. Her devotion was exhibited as an Irish Catholic Christian. He had hoped to turn her but having failed he made her life as miserable as Saint Philomena. Which seemed to appeal to her sense of devotion. Sure, wouldn't she get her reward in heaven, up there with the good Lord and all his saints and apostles? It struck me as a good thing, for she got no obvious or outward reward in her earthly state.

His tongue, the flagellation she appeared to crave. Though, my brother Declan did say, he thought there was more physical flagellation going on in their house. You might recall, my brother Declan went to live with her when he got Annie up the spout. Their sojourn with Evelyn and Ralph was bruising and brief. Ralph having taken to calling their new born "Rosemary's Baby" after the 1968 psychological horror movie, despite both mother and baby being called Evelyn. Declan, having threatened to punch Ralph's lights out, if he slandered mother and child one more time had to leave.

No doubt, you are asking yourself why I am telling you all of this. It's because last Easter he and my Aunt Evelyn came to stay with us. An English man on the Falls Road at the height of the Troubles. Staying in our house. My Da had already had a run in with representatives of the new order. Not only that, Uncle Charlie, who had gone over to the dark side, was now rumoured to be a quarter master in the IRA. If it was true my Da said, the volunteers would have to buy their own guns. Ralph, having a mouth on him which seemed to engage with his brain on selective occasions, was to say the least, a potential recipe for disaster. While those close to us and some neighbours knew him from previous encounters, it was not yet widely known he was related to us. This had good and bad aspects. In the first instance, they might take him for a Brit and shoot him, without making the connection back to us. Good. On the other hand, they might think he's a Brit, shoot him and make the connection back to us. Bad. Though, in both scenario he would be dead, which my Grandad thought was the best outcome we could hope for.

Don't get me wrong, my Grandad wasn't a mercenary man. He came from Anglo Irish stock himself. Protestant landed gentry, two and a bit generation back. In Cork of all places. Among our family were distinguished servants of the great English empire. How we ended up as peasants in a small terrace street off the Falls Road is a tale of lust, love, deceit, debauchery and loss reminiscent of a Victorian penny novel. I will not bore you with the detail. Suffice to say my Grandad took the whole thing to heart, in particular, the fact it was an English man who started the rot leading to our downfall, some one hundred and fifty years earlier. Memories are long in Ireland.

It was with all of this in mind, my Da suggested we get Ralph out of town to a safer space. Why he thought taking an English man across the border to County Cavan was a solution is bereft of understanding. The pretext for doing so, Ralph was a keen fisherman. Cavan being renowned for its fishing lakes seemed a good choice and easy enticement. 'Surely there's as much chance of them shooting him in Cavan as there is here,' I said. Cavan being a border county full of sedition and double barrelled shotguns.

'Don't shit where you eat,' was all my Da said.

County Cavan, was another of the three counties we had stolen from the Ulster Scots. Or so they claimed. They seemed to have forgotten they stole it from the Irish in the first place. The Plantation of the 16th and 17th centuries had seemed to slip their mind. That they had been driven off their own lands by English robber barons and sent to breed in another's nest like cuckoos, had somehow been lost in the mists of time. The same English to whom they now held some sort of bastardised allegiance. An allegiance that led them to go off in droves to die like sheep on foreign soil. Though, some more heartless than me, said not enough of them.

Setting that all aside, we and it was we, because several of us had attempted to persuade, cajole, plead, threaten and entice Ralph to join us on our fishing soiree. The fact, that none of us bar Ralph, knew anything about fishing was irrelevant. It was the intervention of Grandad's oldest mate Gerry that swung it. Ralph, he said, the simple fact is, what these guys know about fishing could be published on the silver paper of a fag packet with room for Shakespeare's book of sonnets. This had its intended effects. It appealed to his sense of superiority as regards fishing. But also showed Gerry as an enlightened and learned man, familiar with the Bart, who represented the great enlightened scholarship of the English. In the end, he agreed to the trip, on the basis of two conditions, his better half didn't go, she was relieved and Gerry joined the fishing party.

On a cold bleak Good Friday, we packed a selection of rods and fishing kit and set our compass for the wilds of Cavan. As none of us could drive, Gerry's son Ronan joined our ranks. His clapped out Austin 1800 being the only transport available to us. My Da insisted on sitting in the front. I slipped in between him and Ronan. Gerry was stuck between my Grandad on the left and Ralph on the right. Which seating positions mirrored their general view of the world.
Good Friday morning was chosen as the pubs were closed.
'By the time we reach Cloverhill the embargo will be over,' announced the Da.
'What is wrong with you people,' asked Ralph as if the decision to close the pubs on a holy day was our doing. 'Not only do you close the pubs on Sunday but in the middle of the week.'
'It's the end of the week,' growled Grandad. 'Start, middle, end what does it matter,' pronounced Ralph, 'it flies in the face of all civilised behaviour.'

'I concur,' cried my Da from the front seat, where he had been pursuing Jerome Jerome's, Three Men in a Boat. 'It's the Puritanical streak in all devout Christians, that drives them to seek ways of punishing the non believer.'

'I think that's a harsh assessment,' countered Ralph. 'Speaking as one of those devout Christians, I take umbrage at being lumped in willy nilly with the weak minded tissue thin zealots who pass themselves off as soldiers of Christ. Like those born again black preachers in America, the word black burning his tongue. The Bible Belt my foot. Praying, excuse the pun, on vulnerable people. All hocus pocus voodoo with their all singing, all dancing Negro choirs. Whooping it up for the Lord.'

'What's the difference,' asked my Da. 'Difference, difference are you mad,' spluttered Ralph.

'We could have a debate about that,' piped Ronan.

'Keep your eyes on the road and your mouth in neutral,' rasped my Da with good humour. 'You go to church, you dress up, sing, pray to the same God. You want the same prize everlasting spiritual life.'

'Everlasting spirits would be more up my street,' joked the Grandad.

'Typical,' spat Ralph, 'To bring the debate back to drink.'

'You started it complaining about the pubs being closed.'

'I did not. I merely pointed out, that in England we are mature enough to decide for ourselves whether to imbibe on holy days. We don't need the State dictating to us the common decency to refrain from alcohol consumption on days of importance in the Christian calendar.'

'Horseshit,' grunted Gerry with a deep sigh. 'Excuse me,' snorted Ralph turning on him only to find him sound asleep, a little dribble of saliva running down his cheek.

'Is he asleep?' asked Ronan.

'Apparently so,' gurned Ralph, 'I would hope, when awake he will refrain from such profanities. I had deemed him a man of culture.'

'Wipe the dribble off his chin will you before it gets on his shirt,' requested Ronan. 'He's dreaming about his roses. He puts horseshit, sorry manure on them. Does them the world of good he claims. He told me that you should call a spade a spade.'

'I have done that,' hissed Ralph.

'Anyway he says pure horse… stuff is better than mushroom compost. More concentrated, full of goodness he claims.'

'I will have to take his word for it.'

'You're not a man of the soil then Ralph,' asked my Da knowing it was a touchy subject.

'I am not!'

I sat mouth shut, as the old and the wise sparred. Throwing little jabs, feigning one way, going the other. The odd left hook thrown but missing its target. Like a Saturday night drunken brawl outside Franks chip shop. If Tommy Ward had been here, he could have given them lessons in the true art. I suspected as the days wore on, it would become more of the eye gouging, head butting type of fight, there would be no Queensbury rules.

The army, actually the UDR, stopped us outside Portadown. Not unexpected. A car loaded with men, the roads quiet. They thought all their Christmas' had come at once, stopping a vehicle full of west Belfast men outside Portadown, a town not known for being liberal.

They hauled us out on the side of the road. Thankfully, we were in sight of quite a large housing development. Who knows what might have occurred, if it had been an isolated spot.
They kept us on the pavement for an hour and a half, small mercies the rain held off. Boot, bonnet, bags opened and examined, as were our live's. We were quizzed about where we were going, coming from, what we did, where we worked, what school I went to. Ralph tried the chatted English man approach but as they were all staunch Northern Unionists, a traitor English man among our taig ranks, wouldn't cut any ice with them. When he started to complain, my Da told him in no uncertain terms, to zip it. He was on our turf now. The rules were different.

I recall years later, being stopped on the Queens Bridge, heading into the east of the city. The UDR soldier, asked my friend who was driving to open his boot. Climbing out he began to undo his boot laces. The UDR Corporal thought it was hilarious and left us standing on the bridge for two hours in the rain, while they carried out other random car checks. Good night, he said, as they piled into the Land Rover and drove off. The one hanging out the back door giving us the V sign.

Being in no hurry, we stopped in Armagh at the archway café, located on its fine Georgian Mall. Passing the Armagh Observatory on the road in. My Da wanted to take an hour to visit the County Museum, which houses a collection of John Luke painting but it was closed. He then suggested the Robinson Library, which has a copy of Gulliver's Travels by Jonathan Swift. There were no takers, each of us finding a point of interest in the cafe to study, while he in turn studied each of us. Keen to instill us with some culture, my Da, as was his want, gave us a little bit of the history of the City. The morning had brightened and we stood with our coats like shrouds wrapped around us, as he sat talking on a bench that had seen better days. Grandad and Gerry we left in the back seat of the car, sleeping head to head. 'Do you think it's safe to leave them there,' asked Ronan.

'I don't think it's very likely anyone will steal them,' sneered Ralph. 'We couldn't be that lucky.'

'I was thinking more they might wake up confused, maybe wander off.'

'The first likely, the second is wishful thinking,' cracked my Da. We all laughed, even Ralph but his was a knowing laugh, always tainted with the feeling, he was laughing at you not with you.

The Armagh Mall is a fine example of a public space. Once common lands, it evolved into a multipurpose site. Initially, it was used for horse racing, cock fighting and dog baiting but Bishop Robinson put an end to that. In later years, it was developed into a fine Georgian park for promenading. The houses fronting on to it are mainly Georgian and behind them is the Royal School, founded in 1608, built at the foot of the Church of Ireland Cathedral.

Armagh is from the Irish, Ard Mhacha meaning height. It's the county town of County Armagh and a city, being the ecclesiastical capital of Ireland. It is the seat of the Archbishops and the Primates of All Ireland for both our lot and the Church of Ireland. In ancient times, nearby Navan Fort (Eamhain Mhacha) was a pagan ceremonial site and one of the great royal capitals of Gaelic Ireland. Today, Armagh is home to two cathedrals both are named after Saint Patrick.

I picked a focus point somewhere just over my Da's left shoulder. This gave the advantage of looking like I was listening, while taking in the Mall behind him. I could see the old prison at the top end through the fine stand of deciduous trees, that lined the boundary of the Mall. A line of school boys, decked out in burgundy and blue blazers, adorned with Just William caps, threaded their way by us, crossing the road they disappeared down the side of the County Museum.

'If we walked to the end of the Mall,' continued the Da, 'we would be able to see St Patrick's, the Catholic Cathedral. The two of them eyeing each other with menace At this stage he had clearly lost his audience. Ralph stood head down, almost Churchillian in his stance. It seemed to say, never in the field of human conflict have so few had to listen to so much. Ronan was inspecting with great intensity, the content of his right ear, which he had extracted with his index finger. Satisfied it was of no importance he cleaned it off on his trouser leg, then smelt his finger. He was the sort of man who would pee, fart and blew his nose in the shower, if he had a shower, which was unlikely, as bathing in dirty water was still all the rage in the 70's.

Side by side they looked Laurel and Hardy. Ralph rotund, his broad round face making his moustache look a bit Hitleresque. The oversized suit jacket he insisted on wearing on special occasion, designed to disguise the belly. Ronan small and thin like his dad, had an almost comical aura. Standing, with one foot on the bench, his brightly flowered shirt with matching neck scarf and green flared trousers made him, sort of Bill and Ben. Flobbalob came to mind. Leaving Armagh we took the Middletown Road but turned off at the sign for Tynan.

'Where are we off to now,' enquired Ralph, 'one of your magical mystery tours Francis.' 'More an educational diversion,' replied the Da.

'Some of us are in need of culture,' snapped the Grandad.

'We have been trying to culture you for five hundred years with little result,' retorted Ralph.

All present did their best to let that one slide, though later it and one or two other such comments would push, at least one in the party, to lose the plot.

'I am taking you past Tynan Abbey, it's a neo gothic romantic country house. Though, one visitor said it was a fine specimen of bastard and vile gothic architecture. It was built around the 1750's to replace an earlier house called Fairview. Its home to a couple of your lot, the Stronge family. They once owned 8000 acres. The main reason for the detour is because this delightful country landscape you see, was once a hotbed of violence, dissent and bloodshed. It was claimed by the local rector, I think his name was Maxwell.'

'Maxwell Silver,' tittered Ralph, 'I knew it was a magical mystery tour.'

'Robert Maxwell I think. In a pamphlet he published, he claimed 150,000 Protestants were murdered in these town lands.'

'Wasn't near enough,' mumbled Gerry, despite his pretence at being asleep.

'The figure was nearer a thousand,' continued my Da. 'Hundreds of Catholics were killed in reprisal. The real significance of Maxwell's pamphlet was Cromwell used it as his excuse to invade Ireland.'

'Your point,' asked Ralph as if that wasn't point enough.

'My point....'

'His point is Ralph, that the English were a shower of lying murdering bastards then and they still are today,' intervened Grandad.

'That's outrageous,' snapped Ralph.

'Someone's going to die before this trip is over,' whispered Ronan to me, the look of a villain on his face.

'My point is,' continued my Da over the mumbles of dissent emanating from the rear, 'nothing in Ireland is what it seems. We layer our history to suit our aims.'

We crossed the border near Glaslough, skirting another fine Anglo Irish estate, Castle Leslie. Home to the Clan Leslie. Another 1000 acres of Irish land, probably bequeathed or gifted to English lords by English royalty, impressed by their ability to slaughter Irish men, women and children. Times change but human nature doesn't.

'Why don't the English get it, that they are not welcome,' pronounced by Da. 'Not because they are English but because they believe their bloody empirical past, using brute force and murder to subjugate people's, was somehow a good thing for those peoples. That somehow, what they did and took, was more than adequately compensated for by what they brought and left. In Ireland, what they brought and left was the cuckoo Planter. What they did and are still doing to their nearest neighbour, is maintaining an artificial divide. Wrapped up in the pretence, that it is the democratic choice of the people. Maintaining the lie fifty years later by brute force and murder.' That our own roots were those of Planters, was being conveniently glossed over. As he said, nothing in Ireland is what it seems.

Ralph seething, had attempted to interrupt his flow but my Da squeezed the words out like bullets from a GPMG. As the last bullet pierced Ralph's ripped, torn and blood soaked body, my Da announced we had arrived at our destination.

'This looks like a grand spot. It came highly recommended. Aggys neighbour Danny, does a lot of fishing in this area and this is where he stops over. It belongs to a Miss Murdoch, a spinster women. Church of Ireland but we will forgive her that indiscretion.' He declared magnanimously.

'It looks expensive,' whined Ralph.

'It's a B&B for Christ sake not the Ritz,' shot Grandad.

My Da and Gerry rapped the front door and entered, leaving us standing on the driveway, each avoiding the others look. Ronan, leaning against the car lit a fag. Sucking on it like a baby at its bottle. My Da had banned him from smoking in his own car.

'Kill yourself if you want but don't be poisoning us, do you not know those things cause lung cancer,' he chastised Ronan.

'You're talking out your arse,' Ronan had spat back. 'My Doctor, Doc McCausland smokes twenty a day. If there was a problem with them, sure he'd be the first to give them up.'

The smoke from the cigarette wafted around his head like a great murmuration, stealing his life and vanished like the Pimpernel.

It was a fine house, its gardens well stocked and tended. The drive was lined with a mixture of rose bushes. None yet in bloom. The house itself was built of stone. Big solid rough cut blocks, the window openings framed in red brick. It was two storey with an attractive hipped roof in slate. There were two attic window to the front. The front door consisted of two large oak doors with matt black ironmongery. The knocker was a lion's head. My Da told me later it was an old Church of Ireland rectory. Miss Murdoch was the daughter of the last minister of the local church.

I broke off from the others, leaving them glaring at each other. The path at the side of the house, was gravel bordered by a range of low plants and small shrubs. I tiptoed on the crunching metamorphs, conscious that my wandering might be deemed nosiness. I liked to think of it as the curiosity of the young enquiring mind. Spinning that line had on one or two occasion got me off the hook. On most, it got me a slap around one ear with the rebuke smart Alec ringing in my other functioning ear. Turning the corner a garden opened up before me, a beautiful expanse of meticulously cut lawn, with uniform stripes running down to a lake shore. The stripes, like a two tone green striped floc wallpaper I had seem in Castleward. The stripes being alternate shades.

I was stunned by the scene before me. It was a masterpiece, wrought by the hand of a genius, Capability Brown eat your heart out, I thought. The old masters would have struggled to capture such perfection. At that moment land, light, water, sky even the very air stood still in perfect harmony, each one beautifully proportioned and positioned. I stepped on to a paved patio and stared at the vista. The lake, like black polished metal, reflected back the clouds that stopped to stare down. The sky azure blue lay over my head, like a gossamer veil. On the lakes left shore, a stand of ancient indigenous trees stood like seasoned warriors. To the right, green fields, hued brown in places by the plough, wallowed up and down like seductive cleavage. On the opposite shore a miniature wall of grey rock, cragged, cracked and broken stood out against the black water. The line between water and rock knife edge sharp.
My Da is going to love this, I reckoned.

The moment was broken by the cry Martin where the hell you are. I'm in heaven.

Miss Murdoch was not how I envisaged a minister's spinster daughter. Short and dumpy, with a hair bun and piny was what I expect, more Women's Institute than Woman's Own. I was more than pleasantly surprised. She was tall, slim and elegant. Her hair brown, with a natural kink hung shoulder length. Under big blue eyes, below a petite nose, sat a pair of Bridget Bardot lips.

The type men hung on, in more ways than one. Lips to listen to, lips to kiss, lips to deceive a wife, lips to end a life. She wore a light weight round neck jumper, her neck adorned with a fine necklace of small pearls. Her back straight, shoulders up. Honed by comportment lessons, in some well healed school for young ladies of country clergymen. Standing to attention her breasts. I had difficulty averting my eyes. She noticed. It wasn't that they were large, they just seemed, even under her clothes, to be perfectly formed. Perfectly symmetrical. It's hard to explain. Though the feeling in my nether regions wasn't. It was like some natural instinct had been hard wired into my teenage brain. I read many years later, that symmetry plays an important role in how we subconsciously judge beauty. To finish her ensemble, she wore a slim pencil skirt to the knee, her legs were bare. Even the small piny, with a country scene, tied around her nipped waist couldn't distract from the overall picture of womanly perfection.

This is Martin announced my Da.
Pleased to meet you Martin she offered her hand. Taking it I nearly bowed my head like those greeting royalty.

A handsome boy Mr Swallow, I can see the streets of Belfast littered with broken hearts. I blushed. At the time, the only thing Belfast streets were littered with was broken bottles and stones.
Her handshake was light, her skin soft but taut. I detected it was not that of a pampered hand.
I held on a little longer than was normal, she didn't seem to mind. No doubt, she knew what effect she had on men and boys.

'Where have you been Martin we were calling for you,' asked my Da.
'I was out back,' I offered with hesitation. 'You are going to love it Da.'
'What have I told you about wandering into...' She cut him off.
'It's fine Francis.' The word Francis delivered like love from her lips. A little tactic naturally learned to break the will of any man. He smiled the smile of the beguiled.
'Come on and I'll show you,' I said with exuberance, 'it's, it's like I imagined Rivendell to be.'
'A Tolkien fan, I am impressed,' she said.

'From knee high proclaimed,' the Da proud as punch. 'Go out with him I will bring you both a cup of tea.'

I thought he was going to kiss her hand. I forgot to ask where the others had gone. Grabbing my Da's coat sleeve I dragged at him. 'Come on, come on,' I called in my excitement.

We crunched down the side of the house and stepped onto the patio.

'Look at that Da, isn't it wonderful,' I proclaimed like Carter to Carnarvon. It's one of the rare moments when my Da was speechless. He flapped his lips like King George the Sixth, the words you're right eventually stuttering out. Flushed with the desire to point here and there, to highlight this and that, I refrained. Silence seemed more in keeping with the moment. We didn't need words.

Absorbed through skin and senses we could hear and feel the engine of the earth turning over. All its parts in harmony, all its layers of organic and inorganic, it tiers of species, one working in unison with the other, living and dying, so others could live and die for one great big cause. At that moment, even God seemed too small a concept to explain it.

Tea called Miss Murdoch, She brought three cups and a plate of buns. Let's sit she proffered. We hadn't noticed the table and upturned chairs. Up ending them, we set them down on the patio in a semi-circle facing the lake. Producing a cloth from her piny. Let me do that, he said, taking it and wiping the table and chairs. With tray placed, we took our seats. I twisted mine a little left so I had a better but hopefully, inconspicuous view of Miss Murdoch.

'I'll be mother,' she said. 'Have a bun Martin, I made them myself'.

My Da while not having a sweet tooth, "I'm more a savoury guy," he used to say, helped himself. It was delicious. Its base, a pastry cup, was filled with strawberry jam on top of which sat a soft sponge cap.

'I assume the jam is also homemade,' mouthed my Da.

'It is, if you like I can show the walled garden where I grow the fruit. It's not grand, walled garden makes it sound stately home. It's very modest.'

My cup had a picture of Queen Elizabeth and Phillip on it. A royal wedding memento.

'Was that insensitive of me,' she suddenly asked.
'What?'

'The cup. My mother was a big fan of the royals. The house is full of coronation and royal wedding cups, bowls and plates.' She laughed.

'Not at all Miss Murdoch,' confirmed my Da.

'It's Christine,' she said the word like a tongue of fire. I thought my Da was going to melt.

'Sure my Ma's a great fan of the Virgin Mary,' says I, 'the place is coming down with holy trinkets.'

My Da looked at me sideways.

'She's a believer then?' she asked the question framed like one from a disbeliever.

'I wonder did the others find the place,' enquired my Da, driving sheep onto the road of conversation to create a diversion.

'Where. Where have they gone?' I enquired.

'The pub,' he huffed as if the very notion was anathema to him.

'Did you not want to go with them Da,' I asked to create mischief. 'Are the pubs not closed on Good Friday?'

'Not our local.' I told them to knock on the side door. Mention my name. To tell Joseph they are staying here. It's only up the road a few miles. I better get back to my chores. A woman's work and all that.'

'Can I help you with anything,' asked my Da. You could have used his tongue to mop the kitchen floor.

'No Francis, thank you. Stay here enjoy the view. But Martin, you can help.'

I nearly leapt out of the chair. 'No problem.'

'Well, pick up that tray and follow me.' My Da grabbed another bun.

I did as bid, following her through the patio doors. The rear view was just as enticing as the front. The rear view of the house I mean of course. Traipsing after her, like the faithful pooch, eyes wide, mouth dry, I waited her command.

'There's three other couples staying, so we need to set four tables for the breakfast in the morning. I'll do one setting to show you.'

I just nodded. If things go as well as they did on the journey down, we might have to set up three extra tables, spaced well apart, I thought. God knows what will happen when they get the drink on them. I followed her instructions, while she went off to do other jobs.

'I have given you and your Da a back room, she announced on her return, it looks directly over the lake, I hope you like it,' she added placing her hand on my shoulder.

'I'm sure I will I stuttered out as the electricity zipped through my body earthing itself in the floor. I imagined if I was to look in a mirror my hair would be standing on end.

'You're shivering Martin,' she observed, 'have you a fever.' She placed her hand on my forehead. Fever I had a fever alright like the one your man Elvis Presley had.

'No I'm fine.'

'Well you haven't got a temperature. It would be terrible to come all the way down here and have to stay in bed.' Her words, while spoken in a quite off hand manner, sounded to me like the sirens call. Each letter, of each word, like soft sensual fingers roaming over my body.

'I'll be fine thanks.'

'Good. Go and tell your father the room is ready he can put the bags in now.'

'I'll do it,' I offered.

'Down the hall,' she pointed, 'turn right at the top of the stair and it's the second door on the left.'

I trotted off finding all the bags stacked in the hall. Extracting ours I made my way upstairs. It was a grand interior. The hall and staircase walls were lined with three quarter height wooden panelling. I was told later it was Irish oak. The grain highlighted by wax. The balustrade ornately carved with ormolu swags, the varnish finish almost translucent. The same wood made up the steps and rises, which were partially covered with a ruby red patterned carpet. The carpet laid with gaps on each side, tethered to the staircase with brass stair rods. Above my head, deep cornicing depicting vines and acanthus leaves. On the walls real art hung. At the top of the stair two portraits, one a large oil, the other a water colour. The oil was of a minister, adorned in his black robes and white clerical collar.

It wasn't bad, a wandering or local artist earning a crust. One of those painting were the eyes follow you wherever you stand. I did a few shimmies left and right to prove the point. The overall pose one of self-importance. A man, chosen by his God to do his earthly work, to lead his flock. To shepherd them to his better world, out of the den of iniquity he created, on purpose or in error, remains the burning question. Uncompromising, the fire and brimstone stare. Dedicated, desperate to impress his maker.

The full figure was seated. One hand and arm resting on a table to his left. His right hand on his knee. Under his left hand, the King James Bible, opened at a

Genesis 1:12. I discerned on closer inspection, though, I couldn't make out any of the other text. On the table books about plants. Oddly, in the bottom right hand corner, a black bird sat on the floor looking up at him. It seemed an odd addition to a serious portrait.

The watercolour, unmistakably was Christine's Mother. There was no mistaking the holy trinity of eyes, nose and lips. I avoided looking at her chest, she was an oul one after all. The clothes and hair were 1950's I guessed, based on pictures of granny and aunts. Obviously, as the wife, the woman, she got water while he got oil, but it was well executed. She had the same set of pearls around her neck. There were no rings on her fingers. I checked the minister, he had one, which my Da told me later was an Ordained Ministers Ring. The oil was slightly out of skew with the other, so I moved the left corner of the frame down a quarter of an inch. Standing back to admire my handy work, I noticed the sitters were sitting back to back. Her look one of wistful distain.

Leaving them both to hang, I made my way down the hall to the second door on the left. The door ajar, I bumped my way in, nearly taking chips out of the woodwork with my Da's case, which was made of wood. It wasn't really a suitcase. It was a joiner's box for carrying his tools. Beautifully constructed with interlocking mitre joints, two brass clasps and a thick handmade leather handle. The letters, JBS, carved into the wood just above the handle. Highlighted in gold paint. Despite its battered appearance it was a thing of beauty, wrought from nature's bounty. Wood, metal, leather. Even the glue was made from animal fats. Setting it down, I placed my plastic Gola kit bag on top. The future resting on the past.

The room was big, certainly bigger than I was used to. Twin beds rested against the door wall. A wardrobe to their right, a chest of drawers with mirror top on the right. Each bed had two pillow. Luxury. I sat on the one nearest the door, apprehensive I might cause the neat prairie like blanket damage. I had never seen a bed with the sheet partly folded over the blanket before. Rising, I soothed my impression from the blanket, it felt like I was eradicating my existence. So going to the end of the bed facing the window, I sat down again squirming a little for extra effect. From there I could see the far side of the lake with its stony outcrop. Only the helmets of the tree warriors were visible. Moving to the window, the light having changed, the lake seemed a little restless. Small ripples like Zebra stripes lay on the surface. I looked back briefly at the ripples I had created on the blanket. On the patio below sat my Da. He was reading. Recently, he had taken to some writer called Hemmingway. A chauvinist pig he told me but boy did he live the life. He said he would leave me his copy of The Old Man and the Sea, as I was still too young to comprehend its importance. He explained it was about an old man pursuing some big fish. I told him I knew all about fishing. That raised a smile.

Back down stairs there was a commotion. I wandered down. The others had returned from the pub. A discussion was raging over the sharing arrangements. Ralph insistent he wanted a room to himself. My Da, Hemmingway stashed in pocket, had come in to act as an adjudicator.

'There is no way I am sharing a room with him,' snarled Ralph.

'The feelings mutual,' spat back Grandad.

'There are no more rooms. The house is full. It's only for three nights. Could the Paddys and Sassenachs not call a truce for three days,' pleaded my Da. 'Don't let ourselves down in front of the southerners.'

'A general ceasefire,' piped up Gerry sarcastically, the hound of Hades under his collar. 'If the RA can do it surely men of peace can.' 'You heard him in the car, and he was at it again in the pub. You, you did it on purpose didn't you,' scowled Ralph, suddenly turning on my Da. 'Now hold on one minute.'

'It's always you at the back of it, with your sarcastic jibes, your intellectual brow beating. Well read, well informed but not well meaning.'

At this point all hell broke loose. My Da making a lunge for Ralph. The others, like GAA refs blowing their whistles, while letting the players cut the tripe out of each other. Handbags at noon, was how Ronan described it later to my Ma. The only real victim being oul Gerry, who in the thick of the melee got knocked over the suitcases. Thankfully, his falling brought the fisty cuffs to an end, as all assisted in up righting him but the verbal recriminations echoed on. At this point Christine appeared.

'Is there a problem Mr Swallow?'
'No Miss Murdoch just some confusion about the sleeping arrangements. Mr Casey here, thought he had booked a single room. But we have sorted it out. He is moving in with Martin,' he announced, his face deadpan. Mine was like an episode of Coronation Street full of angst and northern pain. Ralph smiled. She frowned.
And that's how I ended up sleeping in a little annex room, on a put me up bed, next to Miss Murdoch's bedroom. With a connecting door.

That evening she made us tea and sandwiches, which I helped to serve. The other guests had arrived. A young couple from Derry where stationed next door to Ralph, my Da having moved in with Grandad.

The other guests being two German fishermen and two Dublin lads. While the fishermen had twin beds, the Dublin boys were in the one bed but more about that later.

After tea we retired to the pub. Given it was a holy day the place was banging. Ralph after three pints of stout announced he was not happy about sharing a house with two Nazis and a pair of pufftas.

'Well, I am not happy about sharing a house with an imperialist, racist, homophobic windbag,' piped Grandad.

'I assume you are referring to me.' Nobody disabused him.

Grandad went to the bar.

'Look men could we not call a truce tonight,' pleaded my Da.

'What like a Good Friday agreement,' suggested Ronan.

'Nice one,' chirped Gerry. 'We haven't had one of them before, we can add it to the pile.'

'I'm serious,' moaned the Da. 'Even if it's only for a few hours.'

The others muttering, nodded agreement. A virgin truce descended on the table, like the Holy Ghost descending on Mary.

Various topics were touched upon, including a potential fishing trip the following Easter, Liverpool's recent success. Even the twentieth anniversary of the Queen's coronation got squeezed in quietly. All in aid of the entente cordial.

Grandad having remained at the bar counter for twenty minutes, while all of this passed, was on his return oblivious to the new Anglo Irish accord.

'The barman's a geg,' he announced, 'he says to me why wasn't Jesus born in England because God couldn't find three wise men or a virgin living there.'

That was it, the peace was over. The heavy weapons buried were dug up and thrown on the table.

'Ah f...feck it,' whined my Da 'What?' said Grandad.
'Nothing,' retorted Ronan.
My Da got up and headed for the loo.

'Let me tell you I am a born again Christian and an English man and such profanities are....' 'Exactly,' mouthed Grandad cutting Ralph off, 'I couldn't have put it better myself.'
Ralph ignoring the response ploughed on.
'As such I treat all people equally and fairly.' He took another draught of his pint. His eyes were swimming but in different directions.
'You mean we are all equally beneath you and all fair game,' countered Grandad.
'You are con, con, contorting my words,' slurred Ralph, 'my Christmas fete and Angalis up bringin is is is foundominal till my my being. I am a min of piss and..'
Whereupon he fell forward his head striking the table with a painful crack.
'Good quality wood that,' offered Ronan, 'they don't make tables like that anymore.'
'What happened?' I asked.
'Must have fainted, suggested Ronan. 'It's warm in here alright.'
'Fainted me arse,' chirped oul Gerry, who up to this point had been sitting like chocolate wouldn't melt in his hand. 'I told the barman to throw a wee tipple of Poitin in his pints. It's a hundred proof near.'
'Should we put him in the recovery position,'
I asked.

'We better do something with him he's taking up space on the table,' grumbled the Grandad.

Catching him under the arms, two of them lowered him down on the floor, sort of pushing him under the table with their feet.

'Is that man alright?' asked a local at the next table.

He's English was the response.

Soup drinker shouted someone at the counter.

On my Da's return, he asked about Ralph and was directed to the heap under the table.

'They don't realise how strong Stout is these foreigners. They are used to that oul soapy warm bitter, sure camels wouldn't drink that piss water,' advised Grandad.

'I'll not ask,' said my Da.

Anyway the crack was good that night. A couple of fiddlers arrived and knocked out a ream of tunes. Some local girl sang Come Back Paddy Riley to Ballyjamesduff. There wasn't a dry eye in the house. When she finished with

Machusla, Machusla, I thought some of them were going to throw the rope up. Pining for young ones gone over the sea and oul ones under the sod.

With the help of Joseph the barman, who turned out to be from Bawn, over the county border in Monaghan and who knew my Uncle Jim and Aunt Peggy, we got Ralph in the boot of the Austin. 'We'll see you tomorrow night,' shouted my Da out the window.

'Not if I see ye first,' cried Joseph.

Thank God there were no turns on the road, given Ronan was in no state to walk, never mind drive.

On returning to the B&B, all of us, chastised by the Da to be on our best behaviour, slipped off to bed.

Ralph forgotten and forlorn was left in the boot. All said the next morning it was a pure oversight, the drink having impaired their minds. I had no excuse.

Miss Murdoch was not convinced. Nor were the other guests impressed, when Ralph appeared at the breakfast room door in a ghostly and dishevelled state. I think some formed the view, Miss Murdoch was keeping a house of ill repute. My Da told the gathered he was English. That seemed to satisfy all bar Christine. Profuse apologises followed and she relented. She did point out he could have died of hypothermia and the Garda would have had some difficult questions for her.

My Da, having learnt about the Poitin, told her, given the amount of alcohol he had imbibed, there was more chance of him going on fire spontaneously than freezing to death.

She confessed to me she saw the funny side of it but not in front of the others. I don't want to encourage their childish excesses she said. She told me in her experience, based solely on running the guest house, grown men getting away from home often revert to childhood. Putting her hand on my cheek she told me to keep an eye on them. Given the touch of her hand, which seemed to warm my whole body, I would have killed them had she ask me at that point to do so.

With Ralph tucked up in bed, the notion of fishing was consigned to the waste paper bin. My Da, after a conversation with the German fishermen, who were both called Hans, said he was going to take a couple of hours and walk the local highways and byways. The other three, in the pretence they were going to scout out some good fishing locations, left with grins on their faces like the Milky Bar Kid.

'I know what locations they'll be scouting,' offered Miss Murdoch, 'The Anglers Rest, The Trout & Fly, The Fish & Duck. It's their whistles that will be getting wet, not their feet,' she added. 'Each to their own,' replied my Da. 'Are you coming with me,' he asked.

'I think I'll walk the lake Da,' I proffered.

'Make sure you stay away from the deep bits,' he warned. 'I don't want to be going home to tell your mother Martine is sleepin wit di fishis.' 'Stay on this side of the lake,' advised Christine, 'the rocks on the far side can be treacherous. That's the deep side.'

'I'll be careful,' I confirmed.

Book tucked in pocket, he strode out like a man on a mission. It wasn't exactly death in the afternoon but I suppose we have to cut our cloth to what best suits us and our circumstances. My Da, preferred to let others do the hard graft, he was happy to live the experience through a little easy walking, words and pictures.

Passing through the patio doors I said hello to the Derry couple, Sharon and Con. He inquired after Ralph. I was tempted to tell them he was dead but stifled the urge and said we expected him to be fighting fit for another session that night. She said something in reply, he laughed but I had no idea what it was. Cork, Derry and North Antrim accents were a mystery to me once a sentence went beyond three words.

I walked to the water's edge. The water lapped at my feet like a cat licking cream. I turned back to take in the house. It was on a more elevated site than I realised. The Derry duo waved, I reciprocated. Travelling to my left, simply on the basis I couldn't see fifty yards beyond where I stood, a line of shrubs running down to the shore blocking my view. Reaching them, I squeezed through, to find a well maintained jetty with a boat tied up. Painted in yellow and blue, she was named Sarah. A small amount of rain water had gathered in the bottom. I climbed on board, the boat like Granny Aggy rocking me gently. I sat. There were no oars.

Daydreaming I was drawn back by the Germans.
Hallo, guten Tag Herr Martin,' called the short Hans.
'You are fish today?'

'Not today, tomorrow I hope. The others they..' 'Ya
ya we hear. Mr Ralph the English Lord, he is bittar?'
'As well as can be expected.'

'Gut, gut,' they said in unison. Auf Wiedersehen.
They made off towards the stand of trees, rods, reels
and kit hanging on every limb. The fish didn't have
a chance.

Lord Ralph I laughed.

Vee hav vays of makin you caught, I mimicked.

One of the Germans turned. Did he hear me, I
thought? I waved.

I remembered that slogan during the war "loose lips
sinks ships." I climbed out of the boat with undue
haste, almost toppling into the water. Back on terra
firma I breathed more easily. I stood a while taking
in the scenery, examining stones, rotund and smooth.
Some speckled with graphite others rippled with
white quartz. Dull grey igneous rocks hard and cold
to the touch.

I was buying time. Giving the Germans time to
invade Cavan, making space in fact, as I intended
to head in the same direction. The sun was at its
highest point, the Saturday turning out better than
was expected. I followed the water's edge, coming
upon the stand of trees quicker than expected. Up

close they soared over me. Big grizzly old men, rooted through age to a time and place. A mixed bunch, some smooth skinned and curvaceous, their neighbour gnarled and rough. Each standing shoulder to shoulder against the tide of man and modernity. Tales they could tell, memories passed seed to seed.

A mix of species. Interlinked, reliant. I walked into the shade, the air cooling. The ground at their base dry and firm. Small twigs cracked under my feet. Debased of light, which only shone through in sharp silver spikes like icicles, the ground was bare, patched sparsely with the odd fern and weedy shrub. Small branches and leaves lay dead and dying. Self-culled by nature. The odd bird hopped from branch to branch. Somewhere a crow or rook, I couldn't tell the difference cawed. The sound trilling through the canopies. The volume increased, as if the canopy was acting like the diaphragm in a loudspeaker. I scanned the branches to no avail. Often a rook or crow would be killed by farmers, trussed and hung on trees, as a warning to others to stay away from crops and fruits. That's where the word scarecrow comes from.

My Ma told me the night her father died, a crow or rook, she didn't know either, came and tapped incessantly on the farmhouse window. Only her, my granny and dying Grandad were in the house. She was in her teens and petrified. My Da said in jest one day, maybe it was tapping Morse code, "I've come to get you for killing my brother, come outside and we'll see how tuff you are." My Ma didn't take the joke well. I'm sure she didn't speak to him for a week. He did say to me it was a bit insensitive of him and he regretted it. I am not sure if he said the same to her. In the old days, there was a hierarchy. Apologising maybe undermined it.

I recalled at twilight great plumes of them would swirl and swoop in the darkening evening sky over Baraghy Lough. Silhouetted like vampire bats, calling out to each other, threatening us, like black leather clad bikers on a sunny Saturday in seaside towns throughout the country. Eventually settling down in black blanket formation in the tree tops.

Kicking the leaves over, I could see underneath them a hive of activity. Hunkering down, I watched tiny ants frantic, as hard backed black beetles scurried for cover, I was oblivious to the chaos I was creating in their biosphere. A small stone caught my eye. Round and white I thought it was a marble. Picking it up, it had what looked like a little star carved on it. I put it in my pocket. Somewhere close by a sharp crack startled me. Springing up, I thought I caught a glimpse of someone watching me, before they disappeared behind a vast trunk. Calling out I moved forward in a sort of zig zag motion. Threading my way between trunks and saplings, the odd bramble catching at my jeans. On reaching the spot there was nothing. Turning, I found myself disorientated, every degree of turning looked the same.

I had gone further than expected. A little panicked I drew breath. What had my Da taught me? I ran through the list. Look for moss on the trees, it grows mainly on their north facing side. See if you can locate the direction the sun is shining from. Check the time on your watch. I hadn't got it on. If all else fails, get your compass out, he had added chuckling. I had laughed at that. I wasn't laughing now. It suddenly seemed a lot colder. The sky, what I could see of it, had clouded over. I stood undecided, on the basis I was lost and moving off without further consideration would probably mean getting lost even more. The moss bit I worked out easily enough, as several of the older trees around me were marked with lines of soft moss on their northern sides. Leaning against one of them on its southern side, I watched for an opening in the clouds. It was quite some time before I caught a fleeting glimpse. It came on my right, around the two o'clock mark. All I had to do now, was work out where the sun was, relative to the house, when we arrived on Friday. The problem was, I had the distinct recollection the sun was directly overhead, when we were sitting on the patio. The truth being, I had no idea what compass direction the house lay in. I decided to do slow turns, tuning my ear for the sound of anything. Maybe ducks honking on the water. Nothing.

'Are you lost,' asked the tiny voice? Just a whisper above the silence. Like words delivered on a breath. Turning left, then right, no one. 'Hello. Who's there?'

'Are you lost?' again just perceptible. 'Yes, I suppose I am. Can you help?'

'It's my fault. I'm sorry. Where do you want to go?'

'Home, well not home to Miss Murdoch's home, it's a B&B. I'm staying there with my Da.'

'Your Da.'

The words came from no direction, they seemed to have no gender, no accent.

'Yes, yes my Father I mean. Could you show yourself, please? It feels strange talking to the trees. What's your name?'

'I will take you home. Martin. My Dad Alex says I should take you home....I'm sorry.'

That's it. I woke to find Miss Murdoch sitting on the side of the bed, hers it transpired. She was holding my hand.

He's back she announced softly. My Da standing at the window turned his face a shade of serious. 'What did I tell you about the water? I told you to keep clear.'

'Francis, Francis,' pleaded Christine. 'He''s a boy just a boy. Let him rest shout at him later.'

My Da throwing back the head huffed and left the room.

'He did tell you to stay out of the water.' 'I did I did,' I whined.

'The German guests found you lying half in the water, beside the boat, did you fall out of it, maybe strike your head, you have a bruise.'

I touched my head, the lump did hurt.

'I'm telling you I didn't go.... well I did go in the boat but.'

She smirked.

'But I got out again, I followed the Hans around the shore to the trees. I..'

'They say the last time they saw you, you were beside the boat.'

'I know but I...' 'Ok, I believe you.'

'How long have I been asleep?'

'Five hours. It's seven o'clock. I have some soup for you.' She rose.

'Thank you.'

She bent down and kissed me on my bruise. It was beautifully sore.

When she returned with the soup I asked about the others.

'They were all concerned about you, even Lord Ralph. I have told them you are fine. They are relieved, because they can now go to the pub with a clear conscience.'

I laughed, my head hurt. She nursed me. I was nearly living the dream, like Andy McCourt working an excavator at Eastwood's yard. Andy as a child had dreamt of driving a digger. His dream was fulfilled. Mine lay hidden in my breast.

'My Da?'

'He has gone with them. I told him to go. To relax, that you're ok. Con and Sharon were asking about

you. She said they are hoping for a boy but after your escapade they'll settle for a girl.'
'I better get into my own bed.'
'Stay where you are for now. I have work to do. I will come back and see you in an hour.'
'I...I thought I...' 'What?'

'Nothing. Thank you.' I wanted to tell her, just her, under oath to say nothing to my Da, to the others. But I bottled it. I snuggled down into the bed, the smell of her perfume lingered on the pillow. The bed soft like that eiderdown I heard my Ma and Mrs Brady talking about. I was enveloped, warm and aroused, yet I must have drifted off.

'Let's have you up,' whispered my Da. 'You've inconvenienced Christine long enough today.' Supported he helped me to the put me up bed.
I woke the next morning at seven, the hunger of Africa on my lips. I could hear church bells. It was Easter Sunday, the faithful were being called to prayer. Only the Dublin boys, Roy and Myles were up.
'Good morning are you feeling better. We were so worried. Weren't we Myles?'
'Yes awfully worried,' concurred Myles. 'Thanks. I feel fine. The heads a bit sore.'
'Oh so are ours. We went to Con Conlon's pub with your father and the gang. Mother of god what a night. I never drank as much Babycham in all my life,' gurgled Roy.

'I know,' sighed the other.

'The pair of Germans, lovely boys, they passed out at one.'

Poitin crossed my mind.

'The crack was a hundred. What a voice your uncle Lord Ralph has. An angel. When he sang The Fields of Athenry, I thought my heart was going to burst, trilled Myles.

'Are you sure it was Ralph, he's English,' I asked the face of doubt on me.

'Oh yes. With a voice like his we even forgave him that indiscretion.'

They were like a pair of Larry Graysons. My brother Gerry would love you two, I thought. Literally love you.

'Eat,' said Myles, 'get your strength back.' 'The scrambled eggs are to die for,' piped Roy.

I sat at the big table facing the window. All was pristine. The drinkers were still abed.

Phyllis who helped out in the morning took my order of eggs, bacon and sausage, basically everything. She never smiled and rarely spoke. You had to guess what was on her mind. It was a bit like charades. A beverage beginning with T.

As I waited I weighted up my options. Tell no one. Tell my Da or Christine or both. Maybe I had slipped and fallen, perhaps the blow made me hallucinate. But it all seemed so real.

My breakfast came with an extra egg. My plate half cleared, the first of the posse arrived. Ronan, wearing the face of the abominable snowman and yesterdays clothes sat down opposite me. He helped himself to one of my sausages. The smell of drink wafted as thick as smoke. It rose off him like steam off the Toreadors raging bull.

New aftershave I said. He didn't get it, the cells in his brain still clogged with alcohol poisoning. Dying in their millions, screaming in agony as the alcohol dissolved them. That's probably the reason people suffer headaches the next morning. It's the combined pain of all those dying brain cells. Tea, the full Irish, double rashers and heaps of toast is all he said, before putting his head down on the table.

Over the next half hour they all appeared in various states of dishevelment and pain, including my Da but excluding Ralph. The fish could breathe easily today. My Da was inordinately quiet. No one volunteering any information on Ralph's whereabouts, so I asked. Hoping his naming would not lead to some maniacal rant or threat of all-out war. No one knew.

Over my shoulder the words drifted, we know where he is, don't we Roy.
'We do Myles.'
The others feeding, or dying didn't get the import of what was said. I turned. Roy finger to lips, nodded my attendance. I followed them out.

'He's in our room,' whispered Myles.

'What a night we put in with him. He was all over us. He's like an octopus,' gushed Roy.

'That being said, I suppose it would not be prudent to make it known we were fraternising with the enemy. If we could get him moved from our bed to his own, while everyone else is occupied, if you get my drift,' winked Myles. I did.

'I'll speak to Miss Murdoch. She will know what to do.'

'You're a diamond,' whispered Roy.

So I did. Between us and Pat, her long time gardener, we managed to convey the sleeping beauty to his own room. Keep it for a rainy day I thought. We passed the Hans's on the way. Poitin they said. We nodded. They nodded. 'Ya, ya,' said the short one.

'Take it easy today,' advised Christine. 'Join me for tea on the patio at one. I believe the weather is set to be nice today.' I thanked her and said I would.

Returning by the breakfast room, the Derry duo had appeared. Sharon eight months pregnant and swollen all over, sat her legs splayed like a sumo wrestler.

'How's the head,' asked Con.

'Better than most,' I said. He nodded his agreement.

'Been there, done that, wore the tee shirt.'

'Not anymore,' snapped Sharon though her tone was soft.

'No. No more. Expectant father now. Responsibilities.' Sharon smiled on him, conveying the blessing of the non-virgin mother. They had it all ahead of them. Life, my Da said, an open ended prison sentence.

I climbed the stairs, Mr and Mrs Murdoch looked down on me. They would disapprove, if they knew their home had been turned into a guest house. Mr Murdoch's pose said, my god's mansion may have many rooms but you are not staying here. I did not stop to stare this time. I was troubled. Entering the annex, I lay on the put me up. My clothes from yesterday lay on the chair next to my Gola bag.

I jumped up, grabbing the trousers I plunged my hand into a pocket. Closing my fingers around it I drew out the stone. I wasn't dreaming, I was there the voice was real, well sort of real. I needed to tell someone.'

'The boat, it's called Sarah, was that your mother's name,' I asked teacup in hand.
'Sarah was my daughter.' 'But you're not, not...' 'Not married?'
I squirmed embarrassment.
'You are right I wasn't married. Sarah was illegitimate, a "bastard" child.'
'I'm sorry I didn't mean any offence.'
'None taken Martin. But you have to understand, back then it was a diabolical sin, a Ministers daughter too. He never forgave me and my mother never forgave him.'
'Her rings. Her wedding ring she's not wearing it in the picture.'

'You are very observant.' 'Or nosey.'

'I prefer observant.' I smiled.

'She took them off.' 'When Sarah was born.'

'No when she died.'

I could have bit my tongue. I wanted the ground to open up and swallow me.

'I'm sorry I shouldn't have asked you.'

'It's ok. I'm over it. Sort off. She was born in 1957.'

'What date,' I asked swallowing hard. 'The 5th. The 5th of July.'

My blood drained.

'I was born on the same date.'

'I know, I asked your Father. He told me all about your mother and her numbers.'

'She says I would make a good priest. I have all the attributes I think she called it.'

'Is there such a thing. Does a man really need a god to make him do good things?'

'My Da would know the answer to that one,' I ventured.

'He might just,' she replied.... 'She died when she was twelve.'

She had read my mind.

'Do you mind me asking how?'

'He took her on the boat, her father. He came and visited on her birthday. He wasn't allowed in the house. They had a picnic on the east shore, below the tree line. After, she wanted to play hide and seek. It was her birthday ritual with him. That was it, she hid and we sought. We didn't find her. We never saw her again.'

'I..I. I'm sorry.'

'She would have been your age now, she was a bit of a tomboy. You would have liked her. With no father at home and a grandfather who could not look at her, maybe she thought she had to be tough. Pretend it didn't matter. But it did, it mattered to her and me.'

'You never married.'

'Who'd marry second hand goods? Someone who couldn't even look after her own child.'

I didn't know what to say. I put the pebble on the table. Looking at it, then at me, her face was troubled. 'It has a star on it,' I said not sure why. Stretching her hand out she hesitated then picked it up.

Closing her eyes, I saw a little tear squeeze itself out under her lash. She rubbed it away. 'Where did you find this,' she asked her tone quite harsh.

'Among the trees.' 'On the east shore?

'Yes. It seemed unusual and when you told me about Sarah I just thought there might be a connection. Between it and her. Between her and me.' She looked up. I am not sure how to describe her look, shock, hurt, annoyance. 'When you said the east shore.'

'We looked everywhere,' she said cutting me off. 'For days, weeks we went out. He was out of his mind with grief and shame. My father said it was Gods will. She was not meant to be. I thought he would kill him. You said between you and her, what did you mean.

'The pebble proves I was on the east shore.'

'She could have lost it before they went there, before the picnic.'

I steeled myself licking my dried lips.

'She spoke to me, it was her who brought me home, to the boat I mean.'

The look of horror on her face scared me.

'Why are you doing this? Why are you being cruel?' She went to rise.

'She said, I will take you home Martin. My dad Alex says I should take you home.'

She slumped back on the seat. Tears were pouring down her cheeks, her face etched with a mix of pain and joy.

'I am sorry, I don't mean to make you cry. I just know it wasn't a dream. I was lost and she brought me home. Is that his name, her father's name Alex?'

She nodded. 'Was his name. He took his own life. He spent a year searching for her. He drove himself insane. My father banned him from the land. The Garda's were called several times to remove him but he just came back. They understood but were just doing their job. He died on the east shore.'

'How?'

'He hung himself.'

The hanging crow or rook whichever.

'They couldn't take him away from her after that. Could you find the spot, could you show me?'

'I can try but it all looks the same.' 'We can try. You and I.'

'What about the others.' 'They wouldn't understand.'

'My Da would and my Grandad. Let me tell them. If they say no then we will go.' Rising she grabbed me kissing my forehead. I felt her tear drops falling on my cheek, they ran down their salty brine reaching my lips.

I found them in the lounge in various states of distress.

'Da I need to speak to you, you to Grandad. I need your help. Christine needs your help.' That got their attention. The others sat up. 'Five years ago. Christine's daughter disappeared on the east shore over by those trees. She spent months looking for her, they never found her.'

'Her daughter...'

Cutting him off I stood by the window pointing. 'Yesterday when I was over there and I was over there, I found this white pebble. It has a star carved on it. It belonged to Sarah. It's the first thing of hers ever found since she disappeared. Christine wants me to go with her, to show her where I found it. I'm going and I need you to come.' For a moment I thought they would refuse.

'It's nearly two, we only have a few hours good light ahead of us,' announced my Da. 'Get your boots and warm clothes. Barry and Gerry you need to stay here. We'll meet on the patio in ten minutes.' They tore off. The Hans's, hearing the commotion and advised of events, offered their services, which were willingly accepted.

Gathered on the patio like the magnificent seven, Pat the gardener number seven, looking like a cross between Charles Bronson and Robert Vaughan. He handed round a couple spades.

'Where's Christine,' I asked.

'She's with Barry and Gerry, I told her we would let her know if we were successful, there's no point her putting herself through it all again.'

At a steady pace, the younger of us made the wooded shore in twenty minutes, the aged ten minutes later. The day's weather had turned a little and in the distance worse was on its way.

'We only have a few hours of light. Given past experience,' he looked at me, 'it's easy to get lost over there. I suggest, when we reach the place where Martin found the pebble, we spread out in a line never more than a meter apart. Martin you're on point till then, we'll follow.'

'What are we looking for,' asked Ralph, 'I mean was she carrying anything else or are we looking purely for...remains... Do we know what she was wearing, the colours, type of shoes things that would give us a clue,' he continued to take the bad look of it.

The Da produced a picture. He passed it around. 'Christine gave me this. It was taken on the day, by her father.'

Sitting in the bow of the boat, her body half turned to the photo taker, a girl on the edge of womanhood looked back. Her smile and eyes in contradiction. The Bardot lips, a family trait, broad and voluptuous, slightly parted, as if she was about to speak, ticked up on each corner. But the eyes were shallow and lifeless. They didn't see the taker. The hair, centre parted, a chestnut brown, her skin pale I thought for a tomboy, though she wore regulation jeans and a plain orange jumper, more in keeping with the persona. A tragedy is all Pat said.

Handing the picture back to my Da, he told me to keep it. As if somehow it might help me. I slipped it into my jean pocket.

I led off. We were lined out like those soldiers you saw in Vietnam. The American ones. Desperation on their faces. The realisation that their task was a hopeless one, unwinnable. Like ours.

It wasn't long until we reached the clearing. I pointed out where I had done the digging.

'That's where I saw...' I stumbled to halt. 'Saw,' asked my Da. I felt their stare.

'Did I not mention I thought I saw someone?' 'No.' 'Or the voice.'

Their faces were a mix of confusion, incredulity, my Da's annoyance.

'What are you not telling us? This better not be one of your escapades, demanded my Da.

'Are we on a wild goose chase? Have you no control over him,' whined Ralph turning on the Da.

'Martin!'

'I was here on this very spot. I found the pebble.'
'The pebble,' huffed Ralph.

'It was hers, Christine said so.'

'A desperate woman who couldn't even look after her own child. I heard the locals in the pub. Her and that man of hers. The child lost and he kills himself. Now she has us like fools following this child around.'

'Shut up Ralph, for once just shut your mouth.' 'You should have told us this in the house. Would have saved us a wasted journey,' blurted Ralph. 'Go on Martin.'

'Ya go on Herr Martin.' Hans the taller puffed out his chest at Ralph.

'Remember the war,' said Ralph, 'we won.'

'I swear if there's another word out of you, you are going to go missing on the east shore,' my Da thundered.

'We could drown him now,' said Pat, 'leave his body floating in the lake.'

'I say bury him in the forest over there that looks like a good spot,' suggested Ronan.

'Hold up,' cried Ralph, 'have you all lost your minds.'

'Yes,' snapped Ronan, 'I've had enough of you.' Ralph moved back putting space between himself and the others.

My Da winked at me. 'Go on Martin.'

'I was here digging around, I heard a branch or twig snap. I turned, there was a figure over there, I pointed. It ducked behind the tree.'

'It,' asked Ronan.

'It happened so fast, I couldn't tell if it was a girl, boy, adult.'

Ralph folding his arms across his chest began to shake his head with that I told you so expression. 'What did you do then?'

'I walked towards the tree but there was nothing there. There was a bird somewhere above me in the canopy. He began to cry. Then I heard the voice, whispering to me.'

'That's how Lourdes started you know,' offered Pat, 'children hearing voices.'

'That's how madness starts,' countered Ralph. Swords were drawn. 'I'm only making an observation. It's a well-known fact the madhouses are full of people who hear voices.'

'What did this voice say,' asked Hans the smaller. 'She asked me was I lost, she wanted to know my name.'

'She. A girl's voice. And you told her?'

'Yes a girl's voice. At least I think so. I told her I was staying with Christine, Miss Murdoch.'

'You think so, so you're not sure it was a girl?' pressed Ralph.

'Did she tell you her name?' 'No.'

'Of course not,' puffed the English man.

'Two,' said my Da holding up the victory sign to him. 'Three strikes and you're out,' mouthed Pat pointing at the English man.

Ronan ran his index finger across his throat and winked at him.

'She said she would take me home. That's all I remember I woke up in the house.'

'You should have told us this earlier. Did you tell Miss Murdoch?'

I nodded.

'Is it any wonder the women is agitated,' said Ralph. 'She's clinging to false hope. How could you do that to the poor woman?'

My Da raised his three fingers.

'You know where you can put that,' snarled Ralph. 'We've been duped by an attention seeker. A fantasist. He's your son alright Francis. It's your fault filling his head full of all that fantastical nonsense.'

Above us the bird cried. A threatening cry, territorial.

'The lights going. We should get back.'

'She's here Da, I swear she's here. We are close, I know it. We need to stay.'

'We'll go back, those that want to help can come back out with Martin and I in the morning.' 'We're meant to be going home tomorrow, I have work the next day,' groaned Ronan

We will come announced the Hans's. 'Danke.'

We traipsed back, with little further talk.

'I'll speak to Christine, tell her the light went on us. That we'll resume in the morning,' said my Da as we approached the patio.

The Dublin lads and Derry duo met us at the door.
'Any luck?' asked Con.

We didn't have to speak.

'Are you going out tomorrow?' enquired Myles. 'If so we would like to join you.'

'You'll be very welcome,' confirmed the Da as he headed for the Kitchen.

'I'd join you,' offered Con, 'but Sharon...'

'I understand,' said the Da, 'stay with your wife and child.' Con understood the import of the words.

'Thanks.'

I stepped upstairs. The Reverent Murdoch scowled at me. How dare you he said. How dare you bring that bastard child back. I gave him the fingers. She's coming back, I swear if it's the last thing I do, I'll bring her back.

I fell on the put me up bed, tears weren't far away. Sniffing manly, I sucked them back in. I'll cry tomorrow or the next day or the next when I find you Sarah. Taking the picture out. I kissed her and put her on the pillow. We will meet again, I whispered. Sleep stole me from the world.

I'm not going to tell you that I dreamed about her or she came to me to guide me, because if I did, I don't remember. All I remember is waking with a boner like the Eiffel Tower. How reality always squeezes in. I had fallen asleep in my clothes. Someone had thrown a blanket over me. Rising, I washed my teeth and face in the shared bathroom down the hall. Peeping into Christine's room the bed was empty. I checked my Smiths boys watch on the side table it was 6:45am. I put it on. Not a mouse stirred. Entering the breakfast room I found Christine setting tables. Phyllis was nowhere to be seen. Maybe she was away taking sign language classes, I amused myself with the thought.

Christine was tired. Dark shadows under her eyes, rimmed red from tears.

'Martin I didn't hear you come in.' She smiled sympathy. 'I'm sorry I should have told your father everything before you went.'

'Was he mad?'

'Oh no. It was you he was concerned about. He was concerned the others would think ill of you. That you were making a fool of them and me.'

'I would never do that. Never.'

'I know. I know that. I believe you. I told him that I believe the world isn't all orderly and three dimensional. There are many layers, many things and places we know little about.   He said you and he are no stranger to those things and places. I knew when you arrived there was something special about you.'

I reddened.

'You connected me to feelings long lost, buried. Confused feelings.'

'I'm sorry.'

'Don't be. They gave me hope. You have given me hope. Even if we never find her, I know she is out there.... I'll get you some tea and toast,' back on auto pilot. Guests to feed, rooms to clean.

I felt miserable. A liar. You see I hadn't told them everything. I couldn't bring myself to tell her the truth. Her child was in some form of danger. Someone, something was keeping her. It wasn't a snapping twig, it was a scream that drew me. I got lost because I ran. I followed the screams. And that damned bird crying above my head. Spitting bitterness at me. She's mine, she mine. I swear that's what it was saying.
Her words, I'm sorry, there was something else wrong. I am sure she wasn't saying sorry to me but to someone else. She had upset someone. Maybe, it was that someone who had given me the bump on my head.

Leaving the room I bounded up the stair bursting into my Da's room. He was sitting at the window. Grandad snored.

'What a beautiful place. It's the tragedy of Ireland that her beauty belies her sorrow,' he said not looking at me.
'Let's take the boat Da, take it to the east shore, beach her there.'
'Why?'
It was a good question.

'I didn't tell you all,' I said in a defiant sort of way.
He put Hemmingway down and looked at me over
his glasses, 'Go on.'
So I told him.
'That's why I didn't want to leave her last night, to
leave her one more moment marooned.'
'Christine knows nothing.' 'Nothing.'
'You did right. Get some breakfast in you, the lights
not up yet. It could be a long day....and night.'

Over the next hour the team amassed. All were
accounted for and supplemented by Myles and Roy,
though their choice of clothing was more bohemian
picnic, rather than find the ghost. 'Hans and Hans, I
need you to row the boat at the jetty to the east shore.
We will meet you there.' Said with such authority
they never flinched.

Even Ralph who had turned up in Barbour jacket and
walking stick never raised an eyebrow. 'Before we
leave here today, I want it understood, what we are
doing has a real purpose, it is no fiction, it is not
based on over active imaginings and it is dangerous. I
am not a man for the mellow dramatic, for platitudes
or over stating the facts.' Those that knew him well,
let that one slide down the slipway to sink. 'If any of
you have doubts then leave now.' They stood their
ground, though I saw Myles gently touch Roy's hand
to give him courage.
We strode out, the Hans racing ahead of us. Eager to
get afloat. To set up base camp ready for our arrival.

We will go at the slowest man's pace called my Da
from the front. Everyone raised their pace.
We arrived just as Hans and Hans touched shore. The
looked perturbed. A debate in German with my Da
ensued. All three heads nodding in unison splattered
with Ja's and Nein's.

'Gird your loin's men there's bad work afoot. Lead
on Martin,' he cried, like William Wallace but
without the war paint.

'Not mellow dramatic,' sniffed Ralph, 'my ass.'

Getting my bearings from a tree stump I passed on
the last occasion, I headed in land. We made haste,
already the sky was darkening. Grey rain clouds
like massed SS infantry rolled in from the west. I
let instinct take me. In an arrow head formation we
ploughed through briar and nettle. Curses punctuated
the air making it fouler. There was a smell of death.
Words of blasphemy and the stomp of boots was all
that could be heard.

The rain started, pit, pat, pit dripping down through
the branches, tapping leaves. Morse code, Zulu
drums, the enemy signalling our approach. The
deluge started a few hundred yards in, drops like
missiles pounded our position. Draw closer shouted
my Da. We huddled in. A mass of soaked bodies.
The wind mighty like galloping horses tore past us,
tearing at our clothes. Visibility was virtually nil.

That's why I didn't see it until it was too late. I slammed into its trunk, my face striking the scissor sharp bark. My body spinning left, I fell on my back. Some of the others fell over me, some threw themselves down. Under its canopy the rain had apparently stopped.

Are we all here, commanded the Da.
A quick head count confirmed the numbers added up.

Beneath us the soil was dry. A hundred years of leaves and natures waste lay below us. The tree, its trunk almost red, was enormous. Beyond the canopy the storm raged. Drops of rain striking the ground like bullets.

'We're save in here as long as there's no thunder and lightning,' offered Ronan, as the first peels of thunder rumbled towards us.

'Big mouth,' blurted Ralph.

Only then I noticed the tang of blood on my lips. I'm bleeding I said.

The bark had cut my face in a long shallow wound down the right side.

'Let me look at you,' ordered Ralph. 'St Johns Ambulance service five years if you must ask,' he said to deflect any dissenters. 'It's not deep, nasty enough though. You might end up looking like that baddie from James Bond.'

'Gold Finger,' piped Myles
'I think he means Largo,' offered Roy.

'Nein, Nein, it was Doktar Nein,' said Hans the taller.
'Doctor No.'
'Ja, Ja, Doktar Nein.'

You had to laugh.
I pressed Ralph's hankie to the wound.
The thunder and lightning ripped and roared above our heads. Blue flashes, the shape of pitchforks made Smurffs of us.
'Is it safe to stay under here,' asked Roy.
'Pick your tree dear,' murmured Myles with a warm smile.
'Was this on the weather forecast last night. Did anyone see the weather?' asked Ronan. Somehow missing the real issue confronting us.
'I think this is especially for us,' suggested the Da
'What have you got us into this time Francis? The occult. Devil worship,' mocked Ralph.
I looked at my Da. If he only knew.
'This is going to sound crazy but hear me out.'
'Crazy is my middle name,' simpered Roy.
I'd seen crazier puff pastries.

'Five years ago Christine's daughter disappeared while having a picnic on the east shore with her father Alex. They came over in the boat.'
The one named Sarah, I added.

'During the picnic Sarah asked to play hide and seek. She was never seen again. All sorts of theories abounded. At one stage her father Alex was a prime suspect. He was the last to see her. In the pub the other night, locals still think him guilty. His behaviour afterwards didn't help. Tearing about the place, always looking for her. Some said an act, others that the guilt was eating him. In the end he hung himself.

Back there on the foreshore. The tree stump we passed on the edge of the beach that was the tree. Miss Murdoch had it cut down? I believe he hung himself, because he saw it as the only way to find his daughter. If she was dead he would meet her in the afterlife.' 'Is she dead do you think,' asked tall Hans.

'I'm afraid so.'

'Why, why do you think that? She could have been abducted.'

'She has and she hasn't.' 'Been abducted.'

'Tell them Martin.'

So I did. Some of them looking at me with disbelieve, the odd one eyeing me up for a straight jacket.

'She said I'm sorry twice, but she wasn't talking to me.'

'Who then?'

'Alex, her father,' confirmed Ralph, 'it has to be.' 'I think you are right Ralph, concurred the Da. Her father. He found her. To do so, he gave up his life and now he can't give her up. All this, this is him. The Hans' told me when rowing over they felt like something or someone was trying to drag them back. But he wouldn't sink them, he couldn't sink her boat and in the end they prevailed.

They nodded, Germanic perseverance won the day.

'What now?' asked Myles. 'We wait.'

'For what?'

'For him and hopefully her.' 'Here?'

'This very spot.'

'I didn't take you here,' I offered, 'I was brought here. I let her lead me.'

'They're not going to believe this one in St Galls,' piped Ronan.

'Or the British Legion,' added Ralph. We sort of laughed and waited.

The storm died away.

'Why here Francis?' enquired Pat.

'The tree we are under is a Yew tree. By the looks of it, it must be five hundred years old.'

'Are you going to tell us ghosts and ghouls live here?'

'And fairies,' added my Da. 'No I'm not. While the tree is associated with death and resurrection there's a simpler explanation. The fruit. It's toxic.

I think Sarah took up a hiding place in the tree. Look at all the twists and turns and crevices.' 'Perfect hiding places.'

I stood up to look. The tree was easily sixty feet tall. Its trunk made up of what looked like thick strands of rope lashed together. The bark, peeling in places was a deep brown with purple hues. Its leaves straight, needle like. The branches gangly and thick hung around it like dreadlocks.

'She ate the fruit. It either killed her or rendered her unconscious and she never recovered.'

'You mean we will find her in the tree,' asked Roy.
'I'm afraid so.'
Myles and Roy stepped back. Pat blessed himself.
'Should we look for her,' asked Pat.
'No we have to wait. We have to wait for her father to release her,' he added, raising his voice. 'To give her back to her mother.'
Turning his head slowly looking at each one of us.
'If you want to leave now please do so. I am not sure how this will go.'
I sat back down. The others gathered in, shuffling up close.
'We're here now,' said Ronan.

'My sentiments exactly,' added Ralph. 'Did anyone bring food?'
Hans the smaller delving into his knapsack produced a long sausage.
Bratwurst. He proffered the offending beast. 'Cut me a slice,' said my Da.
'And me,' echoed Ralph.
'Wir warden noch einen Europaer von ihm Machen.'
The Hans's laughed.

'What, what?
'They say we are all Europeans now.'
'Steady on there,' said Ralph but smiling let the rest go.

'Excuse me,' interrupted Myles, 'this might be a stupid question.'
'Probably,' muttered Ralph.

'If her daddy found her through his death and has kept her here against her will since then. Who was it kept her here before he found her?
Just asking,' he added. We all turned to face the Da.
'You've been holding out on us Francis. Bloody Swallows, ducking and diving, economical with the truth. Spit it out who are you expecting.'

'I told you I don't know what to expect. The tree you're sitting under is old. I said five hundred years, it could be a thousand. These trees hold a sacred place in the history of our land. They are long associated with graveyards. It has been suggested, they were planted in the churchyards next to the graves of plague victims, to protect and purify the dead. They are seen in many societies as a symbol of immortality. What better place than a scared tree to mark her grave. If she is taken from here and buried in consecrated ground, then he will never see her again. So he protects her, coercions, threatens her I don't know.' 'You are wrong, it's not me.' We spun round. He was standing a few feet away. As solid as you or I. The others stepped back. 'Alex,' announced my Da, 'we mean you or Sarah no harm.'

'Are you Martin,' he asked looking straight at me. 'Yes.... How is Sarah? Her voice was so soft and kind, I knew she didn't mean me any harm. But she seemed frightened of something, someone.' 'And you weren't?'

'A little. Can I speak to her?'

'She will be here at two, if he lets her come.' 'Who?' 'The one holier than thou, her grandfather, the Minister. He says, she will never be buried in church ground. The bastard child born of lust.'

'The painting Da on the landing. The black bird at his feet and on the table next to his left arm books about plants.'

'Theophrastus' Historia Plantarum. It was first translated.....'

'Here we go another history lesson,' moaned Ralph, seemingly oblivious to the fact we were talking to a dead man.

'Translated,' emphasised the Da, heading Ralph's lamentations off at the pass, 'into Latin by Theodore Gaza; and published in 1483. Johannes Bodaeus published a folio edition in Amsterdam in 1644, complete with commentaries and woodcut illustrations. The first English translation was made by Sir Arthur Hort, published in 1916.' 'The other book is Herball or General Historie of Plantes by John Gerrard, published in 1597. The book you see on the table is the revised edition of 1927, when the book was rearranged so as to form a garden calendar, the plants being listed seasonally.

'Was he a keen gardener, Francis,' asked Roy. I was convinced the trauma of the situation was beginning to effect the cognitive operation of people's minds.

'No Roy. It was the text of the bible under his hand, that caught my attention, it's the key.' 'Genesis 1:12. "The earth brought forth vegetation, plants yielding seeds after their kind, and trees bearing fruit with seed in them; and God saw that it was good."

Hearing Da quote scripture was a surprise to several of us.
'I looked it up,' he offered in explanation.

'You should have asked me,' said Ralph, 'some of us are familiar with the good book.'

'Are you saying he knew how she died and where she was? He knew and he never said,' asked Myles.
'For him it was gods will. The seeds of the tree did what was expected of them, they poisoned her and he saw it as gods work. Retribution.
In his eyes she was born out of lust not love'.
'She was born out of love and is still loved in heaven and on earth, I said the lilt of Baron on my lips. Please Alex tell me what I need to do.'
I can't confront him. I am tainted with my own death. He will be here. I can't guide you.'
Above our heads the crow or rook, whichever, cried time. Alex was gone, no puff of smoke, no ghostly wobble as he went. Just gone.

'Go, all of you go, NOW, roared the Da. Lead them out Ralph. You have the compass I gave you. West, head west. Don't come back.'

The Hans's looked at him. 'The boat,' he mouthed. They nodded.

They began to scurry, headless at first, until Ralph took charge.

On me, follow he shouted. They moved off, rag tag, some looking back over their shoulders. Catching the last glimpse of us they no doubt thought.

'Was that wise Da? There's strength in numbers.'

We're out of our depth son, I couldn't take a chance with their lives…. You've really done for us this time. We come here for a quiet bit of fishing and you land us in a family feud and worst of all, most of them are dead.'

'That's rich,' says I, 'you were all up for it when I mentioned it.'

'What did you want me to do say no to Miss Murdoch?'

'Don't be giving me that Miss Murdoch bit. It's Christineeee. That's her name Francissss.'

'Now just you hold on there one minute you're not too old to be given a good…'

'Thrashing.' The word came at us blindside. We pirouetted like those mechanical ballet dancers sold in seaside towns.

He was standing fully decked out in his Cossack and collar.

'You wanted to see me gentlemen, you have something to say to me.'

Yes, I growled at him, bearing my teeth, like oul Barney the Bellevue Zoo lion did to the visiting school children, but with more effect.

'Children should be seen and not heard. Control your child.'

'Reverent Murdoch I can't say it's a pleasure to meet you.'

'The feeling is mutual.'

'I was going to say in the flesh but then you are not... flesh. I feel I have an advantage over you as I am still alive, I still have a chance to safe my soul.' 'For now.'

'You would take pleasure in my death.'

'It is the purpose of life. What are we born for but to die in gods light? We should all take pleasure in our death, if we have lived righteous lives.' 'And you lived a righteous life.'

'We are not here to discuss me. We are here to talk about the bastard child.'

'Sarah, her name is Sarah. Your daughter's child,' I seethed.

'I have no daughter.'

'I'm beginning to believe that Reverent. She has none of your physical features. All her mothers. And her temperament I speculate not yours.'

'Your point is.'

'Christine's not your own. She's certainly not adopted. You took the mother on with love and her love child as penance.'

'I didn't know about the child at the time. Women are deceitful creatures, but we must procreate to fulfil the lords will.'

'Someone did it for you. She caught you. A good catch a young Minister with a fine church estate. How many acres three hundred I read and ten other tenant farms. A tidy income. You could have divorced.'

'I made my vows before the altar of Christ. I was not going to bring shame on myself and my church. I could not destroy the child but I did not have to make it welcome.'

'You had no children of your own.'

'How could I, her womb was soiled. And mother like daughter. Another bastard in my home. The Devils spawn. I reared one bastard I had done my penance. I wasn't about to do it again. But the Lord found a way to avenge me, to unshackle me from the burden.'

'Your loving God!'

'A practical one.'

'Who kills children for revenge?' I parried. 'Children get killed every day. He finds   no pleasure in it. Adam cast the first stone killing the world God created for him. So God said to Adam live in the world you created.'

'Someone's lying to us Da,' I said.

'I am the one sinned against. My wife, Christine's mother punished me, so I punish her. That is only fair.'

'But you are punishing Sarah. She did not ask to be born. She was brought into the world through Gods wondrous creation birth. A beautiful child, a happy child, her life blighted and poisoned by the sins of others.'

I knew where this was going. We were going to end up in one of those long and winding theological debates. I wasn't having it.

'You believe in the sacrament of baptism,' I asked cutting across the Da's pontifications.

'Of course.'

'Was she baptised?'

'Yes but not by me,' he retorted a clear smirk on his mouth.

'Then, whatever sins you say she had, they were washed away by her baptism,' chimed the Da taking up my theme. 'A clean sheet. The sins of father and mother wiped away. Pristine and white ready for God to write her story on. Not for you to scratch hatred and malice on. During her short life, can you recount one time or one event when she exhibited any element of disregard for you, your religion, for your position in the community?' 'Did she call you Grandad,' I asked. It was like a stake through the heart.

'I recall she used the term Pa....She called me Pa.'

'And you rejected her?' I spat back.

'I believe what matters, is how we care for one another in the here and now Reverent Murdoch,' interjected my da. After that its Gods will what happens to us. You and your church seem a little too preoccupied by the afters. I am not as familiar

175

with the holy text as you, but I do recall something along the lines, Suffer on to me little children.' "And whoso shall receive one..."

'Such little child in my name receiveth me,' said the Reverent taking up the queue. He continued. 'But whoso shall offend one of these little ones which believe in me, it were better for him that a millstone were hanged about his neck, and that he were drowned in the depth of the sea.....'

'Take heed that ye despise not one of these little ones; for I say unto you, that in heaven their angels do always behold the face of my Father which is in heaven.'

'Matthew 18: 1-10 would have been more appropriate,' suggested the Da. 'Do what Adam did, cast another stone, break your world,' he added for effect. 'Let her go, let her go to your god.'

'I can't, I am beyond doing, I have no control.' 'Tell your god you forgive her. Ask him to forgive you.'

'It is not my god who holds her soul or mine. She was dead, unburied lying between heaven and hell. Uncollected. Until that fool killed himself. He found her and raised her spirit. I had no choice, I had to act.' 'You sold her soul to the devil?' 'No I sold my own. I sold my soul to the devil so that she would never get to heaven. Heaven had no place for her kind.'

At that the Reverent fell to his knees. I won't go into all the woe is me, forgive me lord stuff.

It was like your man on the road to Damascus. That was it. No more thunder bolts and weird goings on, no more bloody big birds squawking in our ears. All the hocus pocus, the holy this and spirit that didn't amount to a hill of beans. 'We will arrange to collect her tomorrow,' offered the Da.

'During the storm, I saw her resting in the crook of two great branches, like two mighty arms had enveloped her. She is at peace now. Remember her as in the picture.'
I just nodded.

'You did well he said, putting his hand on my shoulder. But less of the sarcasm.'

We left the Reverent on his knees beseeching the Lord. I reckoned he had a lot of questions to answer. Not least to my mate the devil, who was no doubt making his way to the east shore as we made our exit.

'I was quite pleased with the loved in heaven and on earth bit,' I said my head swelling.
'Out of the mouths of babies,' retorted the Da.

'I hope you know where we are going,' I asked in childish retribution.

'Simple, as I told Ralph head west. Remember this side of the lake is called the east shore.'

Idiot I thought.

'What do we tell the others?'

'Nothing. Let's just say we waited, no one came and we found Sarah's remains among the branches. A damp squid you might say.'
'What about Alex and the apparitions.'

'The toxic effects of the poisons in the Yew trees rotting fruit. A rational explanation. More rational than the truth.'

'And Christine.'

'We tell her the truth.'

On reaching the shore we found the Hans's waiting. 'A false alarm,' said my Da, plus other stuff in German I didn't understand. The bottom line being, he confirmed we had found Sarah's mortal remains. They are going to row us back he said.

We climbed on board. The two Germans, experienced oarsmen, powered us out into the lake.

'Nehmen Sie den langen Weg,' called my Da. 'I asked them to take their time.'

They pushed us in an arc across the lake. I looked at my watch. It was two o'clock. It was Easter Monday and I never even had an Easter egg.

'You never went to mass yesterday. Your Ma's going to have my guts for garters.'

'I heard enough quotations from the bible today to do me a lifetime,'

'Sarcasm,' the Da reminded me.

'I'll tell her I was acting the lig and fell. Sure take a look at me I look like I've been in the wars.' 'Thanks. In the Easter calendar this day is often called "Bright Monday" or "Renewal Monday, appropriate I think,' suggested the Da.

I noticed he dipped his fingers in the water and surreptitiously touched his forehead.

Till that point I had been oblivious of the vista from the boat. I am not going to tell you that the house on its height seemed brighter, happier, a cloud lifted and all that guff. It just felt that way. Maybe it was because I felt that way.

On the shoreline stood most of the others. Christine among them. The Dublin boys waved gaily, if I am allowed to use that expression. We came to a crunching halt at their feet, several wading out to pull us ashore. Like Jesus coming ashore at Capernaum, I stepped out. Christine hugged me enveloping me in a mothers embrace. She took my Da's hand and thanked him.

'You got them back safe,' said my Da turning to Ralph.

'Did you doubt it?'

'No. I didn't. I didn't doubt it for a moment.' They shuck hands.

We left the pair of Hans sitting on the shoreline sharing Bratwurst. No doubt agreeing, that they were never coming back to Cavan or Ireland again to fish. Too many distractions and crazy dead Irish people.

Christine sat me down on a patio chair.

'I need to look at that cut,' she said. 'Would you like some tea, three sugars?' I nodded.

'And a ham and cheese sandwich please.'

My Da retired to the lounge to fill the others in. Fed, watered and my wounds dressed, I stayed on the patio, while the Da having returned, conversed with Christine. There was some debate as to whether the Garda should be called. The state pathologist would have to examine the remains, before their removal. Christine thought she might leave her where she was. After all, the Yew was a holy tree. Many being found in burial grounds, some even pre-dating the church and churchyard where they stood. My Da said it was up to her. He didn't tell her about the devil. She said Alex would like it if we left her where he could visit. She would visit in the morning. It all seemed sensible.

Doesn't it.

The Derry duo left. I heard Sharon tell Con she thought Sarah was a nice name. Do you not think it's a bit Protestant he remarked.
'Frank our flat mate won't believe a word of it,' said Myles.
'He's a complete atheist,' added Roy as they made their farewells.

'Don't call us we'll call you,' cackled Myles kissing me on the cheek. No offence but you scared the bejesus out of us. He's going to be in therapy for years,' he added, looking back at Roy. They left in a flurry of goodbyes.

Ralph and the three amigos retired to the pub. Their last night of extended freedom. We'll join you later had confirmed the Da.

I decided to lie down for a while, the weight of the weekend's events finally draining me. I threw myself down on a corner settee. In my repose, I saw Sarah on the lake, leaning over the bow of the boat, trailing her hand in the water, it reflecting her mirror image back.

Raising her head, she smiled at someone in the boat. I couldn't see who it was. Putting her hand to her mouth, pearls of water clinging to the finger tips, she kissed her palm.

I was woken by someone touching my shoulder, my Da.

'You're like oul Gerry lying there slobbering in your sleep. Wipe your cheek.'

Sitting up I could feel the smear of damp on my face. I touched it with my hand and kissed my palm. Slobber, do you not recognise the kiss of an angel you oul codger, I said to myself. Of course, it might just have been those stifled tears.

All was quiet. Phyllis had returned from non-verbal communication course, moving about the lounge, avoiding all eye contact with us in case we turned her into a three toed toad.

My Da asked me to get his coat. On the landing I took one last look at the portraits. The Jezebel and Jeramiah. I had to take a double take. Under his left hand the text read Matthew 18: 1-10. The damned bird was still there. Slipping my hand in my pocket I found Sarah's photograph. I tucked it into the corner of her grandmother's picture frame. Then, on second thought I moved it to the Reverend's frame. Forever after, he would have to look on the child he rejected.

Picking up the overcoat, a piece of paper floated down to the floor. Lifting it up, I saw what looked like a rough family tree. He'd been doing his homework in advance of our mission. It was the name Riordan that caught my eye. He had pencilled in Christine's real fathers name, Matt Riordan. Below it with a question mark added, which had been crossed out, the name Alex Riordan. Alex her lover, Sarah's father was Christine's half brother. Matt Riordan was his father. Next to it in different ink his mother's name Sarah Madigan.

I sat down on the crumbled bed. The child didn't stand a chance I thought. Looking out the window, night had enveloped us. A broad line of silver moonlight, cast across the water, was all the illumination present. The ray like a highway to the heavens.

Downstairs I handed him the coat, the paper crumpled up in its pocket. Better let sleeping dogs lie he often said.

Pat the gardener gave us a lift to the pub. As we entered, it wasn't quite like that scene from An American Werewolf in London but pretty close. Pat stayed for one for the road, which turned in to six. The sixth for the hedges. The barman got him a lift with a local going his way.

There seemed to be some discord at the amigos table. The Good Friday agreement sounded like it was in trouble.

'Tiocfaidh ar la,' called Ralph in his best south London accent.

'Ta tu ag do la,' retorted a local wag at the counter. There was uproar.

Peace has always been fragile in Ireland.

Many years later, I picked up a copy of a song called Sarah by Thin Lizzy. I sent it to Christine. The words seemed appropriate. "You are all I want to know You hold my heart so don't let go You are all I need to live My love to you I give.."